Bitter Betrayal

There was no one at the reception desk. Michael believed there should always be a clerk ready to greet customers. It looked like you didn't care if there was no one there. He rang the bell; it seemed to echo out along the corridor. He checked his watch, almost ten thirty... there should have been some guests checking out, or a clerk making up bills, *something* happening, not this feeling of emptiness. The atmosphere was so desolate that he wondered if he was off his head to contemplate buying this hotel. After all, he owned a chain of exclusive hotels and Blooms was hardly in that league, far from it.

He was just about to slam his palm on the bell again when a door opposite the desk that he knew let in onto the office, opened. A tall, slim person wearing a sweatshirt and grubby jeans stood there. There was a baseball cap pulled low on her head, for it was a she. The curves at her chest showed that clearly enough.

"Hi," he said, trying to stem the faint feeling of revulsion washing over him. What was Bloom thinking about having someone like *that* as a hotel receptionist? No wonder no one wanted to stay at his damn hotel. "I'm here to see Charles Bloom."

"Charley Bloom is here," she said, "Mr Hernandez, you'dbetter come through."

Wings

BITTER BETRAYAL

by

Margaret Blake

A Wings ePress, Inc.

Contemporary Romance Novel

Wings ePress, Inc.

Edited by: Christie Kraemer
Copy Edited by: Jeanne Smith
Senior Editor: Anita York
Executive Editor: Lorraine Stephens
Cover Artist: Richard Stroud

All rights reserved

Wings ePress Books
http://www.wings-press.com

Copyright © 2009 by Margaret Blake
ISBN 978-1-59705-380-8

Published In the United States Of America

April 2009

Wings ePress Inc.
403 Wallace Court
Richmond, KY 40475

Dedication

For Kathy O Connor, with thanks for all her help
and support.

One

There was no one at the reception desk. Michael believed there should always be a clerk ready to greet customers. It looked like you didn't care if there was no one there. He rang the bell; it seemed to echo out along the corridor. He checked his watch, almost ten thirty... there should have been some guests checking out, or a clerk making up bills, *something* happening, not this feeling of emptiness. The atmosphere was so desolate that he wondered if he was off his head to contemplate buying this hotel. After all, he owned a chain of exclusive hotels and Blooms was hardly in that league, far from it.

He was just about to slam his palm on the bell again when a door opposite the desk that he knew let in onto the office, opened. A tall, slim person wearing a sweatshirt and grubby jeans stood there. There was a baseball cap pulled low on her head, for it was a she. The curves at her chest showed that clearly enough.

"Hi," he said, trying to stem the faint feeling of revulsion washing over him. What was Bloom thinking about having someone like *that* as a hotel receptionist? No wonder no one wanted to stay at his damn hotel. "I'm here to see Charles Bloom."

"Charley Bloom is here," she said, "Mr Hernandez, you'd better come through."

That was one strike up for her; she knew who he was. She opened the little gate and raised the counter so he could step behind reception, then led the way into the office.

The office was in a real mess, with papers and files littering the desks and most of the area of floor space. There was a filing cabinet, one of the drawers open, files piled high on their holders instead of sitting snugly inside.

"Take a seat," she said, indicating the only chair that did not have files on it. He refused to sit. She shrugged and went behind the desk, but the chair was also cluttered so she perched on the edge of the desk. He wished she would not keep looking down; he hated it when people refused to make eye contact.

"So where is Charles Bloom?" he asked as politely as he could muster. He didn't have all day and his limited patience was fast evaporating.

"What do you want? You had to have heard we weren't selling," she answered in a rather impudent tone of voice.

He had *not* heard. "*We* weren't? Who's the we?"

"Me and my dad."

"Your dad?" He thought he got it. "I didn't know there was a me and my dad."

"There wasn't when you first spoke to my dad, but there is now."

"Oh, yeah? Look, Miss Bloom, I don't have all day. I want a definite yes or no from Mr Bloom. Is he selling or not?"

2

"He isn't selling and neither am I, Michael…"

He threw her a sharp look at her use of his Christian name. She raised her chin, then her hand and pulled off the grubby baseball cap. Long nut-brown hair spilled out, falling in wanton waves over her slender shoulders. She met his stare; her eyes were so familiar, very pale tawny coloured round eyes that were shaded by long thick lashes.

"My God!" The words exploded from him. "Charlotte?"

~ * ~

"I don't believe it," he muttered, impatiently thrusting his hands into the pockets of his immaculate grey silk mohair jacket. He glared at her, pinning her with a hard stare. "What the hell is going on? You're not called Bloom. You're plain old Charlotte Smith, at least that was what you called yourself."

Although knowing she did not have to explain herself, Charley gave him an ambiguous reply. "I was one and then the other and then the other again."

"What are you talking about?" he demanded. His anger was plain to see, yet his anger was also a mask for something else. Other feelings that he did not want to come to the surface.

"I mean, I was born a Bloom, until Mum and Dad got divorced and my mother remarried. I wanted to please her, and dad did not want to know me, or that was what I was told, so I took her husband's name."

"I see." It made no sense to him but he did not want *her* to know that. "So now you want to punish *me* for some crazy reason?" He raised an eyebrow at her, weighing her for her reaction.

"Why would I want to do that?" she asked, her eyes round, yet her cheeks flushed dark crimson, giving away some kind of inner feeling.

Perhaps she was not as detached as she was pretending. Damn the woman to purgatory, but she was still *so* beautiful. Not in the conventional sense, of course, but there was something stunning about all that nut brown hair, those tawny eyes that were ever so slightly tilted at the corners. Her nose was a little too long and straight but her lips were round and full and a luscious shade of fruity pink. She was not quite a tall girl, being about five foot six and neither was she slender, being round at the breast and hip in a delicious way. *A man's woman*, he thought, *very definitely screen siren more than catwalk queen.*

He had stared at her a long time without saying anything and realising that she thought she had somehow gained an advantage, he abruptly broke the silence.

"Who knows? If anyone wants revenge, I guess I'm the one. But I'm not here to discuss that, Charlotte. As far as I am concerned, the past is the past. All I want to do is get on with my business and then get back to London."

"My name is Charley," she snapped at him, "use that or Miss Bloom but don't ever call me Charlotte, because Charlotte, little naïve Charlotte, is as dead to me as the past is to you."

She was giving off waves of anger. He could see that in the way she tossed back her hair … it was meant to emphasise what she said, but it was a very provocative action.

4

"Give me time," he said. "You can't expect me to remember on the spot—Charley—and I don't get your description of Charlotte Smith. She was no little innocent abroad, albeit that she pretended to be." He managed, with a good deal of effort, to speak very calmly, to summon up reservoirs of strength that made him seem cold and businesslike.

"I'm not giving you any time for anything, Michael. Look, you've been told; Bloom's is not for sale."

Her voice sounded really hostile and he could not understand why she should be that way. He had done nothing to her, whereas she—no, he was not going to examine that pot of worms; otherwise he really would lose control.

"So the prodigal daughter has come back to save the business. Hey, sounds like a good movie."

"It could be something like that. However, it isn't any of your business. You were told we weren't interested anymore. Then, of course, you should ask yourself the question: why would I sell to you? *You, of all people?*"

"I guess because I'm the only one stupid enough to buy this place," he said, glancing around contemptuously before turning to her once more. He studied her face... the pale skin, that lovely English complexion that was one of the first things he had noticed about her. He could recall so many things about her... her smell, the feel of her skin ...and realised he had to be out of his head letting his mind carry him away like that. Michael straightened, chasing away the memories. He frowned at her and gave her a contemptuous look.

She was not cowed by it. Instead she said, very clearly and without much emotion, "I'm not selling and I'm the owner now. You're right, I am the prodigal daughter, but as I said, it's not any of your business."

"I'd still like to talk to Charles Bloom, Charlotte, if it's not too much trouble."

"I'd like to talk to him, too," she murmured. Her eyes were ever so shiny. She saw the intensity of his gaze and turned slightly away. "But he died... two days ago."

He was quiet for some long moments, words flashing in and out of his mind only to be discarded. In the end he said, "I'm sorry to hear that," and he was. He had liked Charles Bloom. She had finally knocked the arrogance out of him; he could not call up any more strength nor act a part, not when she had revealed such sad and bad news.

"We had decided not to sell before..." she said, shrugging a little. "He thought I could do good things."

"I'm sure you could, if you have the money," he reluctantly agreed, although it was something of a white lie. He did not think she had the expertise to pull something off like that. She had known nothing about the hotel business in the past; in fact, she had been working at a diner in a small town in New York when he had first met her.

"That might be a problem," she was honest enough to admit.

He had always thought Charlotte was very honest. It was one of the things that he had admired about her; only later did he find out that she was not to be trusted at all. Far from it, she was a cheating little schemer. It was not hard to remember that. In fact, it was difficult to push it out of his mind, but he knew he had to because of the circumstances in which she found herself. He never kicked anyone when they were down, and she was really down at the moment.

"Charlotte," he began, then shrugged and changed his mind. "I'd like to pay my respects, if that's okay?"

"Certainly," she said in a clipped voice, then gave him the details for the funeral.

"I'll be there. See you, Charlotte."

He didn't look back. Quietly closing the door behind him, he went with purposeful steps across the lobby. He had to get out in the fresh air. It was spotting with rain but he did not call a cab. His errant footsteps led him to the entrance of a park. He went inside. It was quiet, just a few dog walkers and mothers with infants. There was a conflict of emotion churning away inside him. Sorrow for the death of Charles Bloom, certainly. The man had to be barely turned sixty; it seemed that it had been a sudden death. Any other time, he would have felt sorry for the man's daughter, only he could not feel anything but fury at Charlotte. Seeing her again had opened up old wounds.

There was a bench close by; he went and sat on it, staring at the row of elm trees, wondering if he would shake it off before his flight back to London. He was over her now. He was no longer the twenty-two-year old with stars in his eyes, far from it. She had seen to that. Charlotte had ripped out his heart and stamped on it. No, he could never feel *sorry* for her. The rage came, soaking up the pain. Then, a determination to somehow pay her back exploded inside him. He was not sure how he could do that, but he was sure he would try. Revenge was the dish best eaten cold; he would enjoy the feast, somehow, some way.

~ * ~

Charley stood as Michael Hernandez went through the door. She felt herself sway a little, and held onto the filing cabinet. There was a rush of something quite potent running through her; it drained away the adrenaline, leaving her feeling weak and helpless. It was there again, that light headed feeling. When she had seen him at the reception desk she had almost reeled; she felt like a Victorian woman swooning away for want of smelling salts. It was ridiculous this effect he had on her. It was a dangerous concoction, for she found she could still feel bitter and angry at him, yet at the same time be physically weakened by his appearance. He was very different from how he had been those dizzy years ago. Now he was a mature man and that maturity sat well on his shoulders. He was even more devastatingly attractive than he had been as a young man. In fact, his physical attraction had quadrupled and that was very disconcerting.

Analyse it, girl, she said, *analyse it, classify it and then file it away.* Yet how could she do that? There was no sane explanation for the way that Michael Hernandez made her feel, there never had been. It had been there the first moment she had set eyes on him. He was young then, boyish, tall and with his broad shoulders, rather angular. She noticed the moment she saw the older version of him that he had "filled out," that he was no longer angular but muscular in an attractive kind of way. His jet black hair, that had a rather tight curl, was cut shorter than back then, but it still had the gloss of a blackbird's wing. His skin was that toasted colour that betrayed his Spanish ancestry. Those dark eyes… long, perfect almonds, the iris so dark that the pupil was barely perceptible. There was Roman arrogance about his nose. When he had been younger, it had seemed to slightly dominate his face, taking away the impression of his being very handsome. However, his features had matured; the nose only served to emphasise his physical attractiveness. Below his nose, his mouth was perfectly shaped, the lips long and narrow but even in youth there was a cynical twist to his smile that she had found rather disturbing. She closed her eyes as the memories threatened to invade. She could not afford to go down that path and not be in control.

Now he was different, not only older and less angular, his features were settled and he was handsome. Time had made him more good looking. It was so unfair. In eight years, he should not have been allowed to become even more devastating than the young man she had met. The young man she had loved and... she gasped, holding onto herself... *left!*

"Dad, she murmured into emptiness, "did you know what you were doing when you brought him into my life again? Did you do it on purpose? Were you playing games with my heart?" She shook her head, roughly wiping away the tears; the tears were for her father and not for Michael Hernandez. How cruel that she had found her dad again only to lose him so suddenly. She looked around the office, felt a sudden burst of fury and resentment. Picking up a bundle of files, she dumped them into the black bin liner she had brought for that very purpose. She had to get on, no matter what, had to get the system up and running. She could not wait until after her father's funeral because financially they were on the brink of ruin.

The solution to all her problems had gone through the door, leaving behind the familiar scent of summer. But no, she was not going to give in. Could not find it in herself to give Michael Hernandez what he wanted; there had been too much of that in the past, Michael Hernandez getting everything he wanted and then when he got it, throwing it away.

The ringing of the bell on reception drove her out of the office. It was the company with the computer. She had no time to mull or to even mope over anything. She just had to get on.

~ * ~

It was a surprise to see that Michael Hernandez kept his word and turned up for her father's funeral. Quite a few people attended and many that she did not even know. The chef at the hotel, who had promised to stay for a couple of months and see how things went, had made a small buffet back at Blooms. She had thought not to have anything like that, but then had changed her mind. She was glad she did, for so many people had good stories to tell her about her father. It was like getting to know him all over again. She had not seen her father since she was very young. There had been an acrimonious marriage breakdown and her mother had wanted to start again when she remarried. Charles Bloom disappeared from her life, but Charley had not known that it was not entirely voluntary. Later, her father regretted that he had not put more effort into seeing her again. People's stories about his life were therefore prized by her.

She spoke to so many people in the small cocktail bar, and all the time was aware that Michael Hernandez had come back also. She felt his eyes following her as she went around the room talking to people, yet when she turned to look at him he was always in conversation with someone else. I'm paranoid, she said to herself. He doesn't care about me and I care less about him. He is being the polite, well-brought up person he always affected to be.

People began to drift away and the girl who had come in to help serve the food began to clear away. Soon there was no one around but Michael Hernandez. He had not approached her to offer condolences as everyone else had. Now he came towards her, the moment she had dreaded, and which was made even worse by the fact that he had waited until everyone else had gone.

Squaring her shoulders and tilting her chin, she stood waiting for him to reach her.

Michael asked. "How are you?"

"All right," she said. "It was kind of you to come." She forced herself to sound gracious.

"I told you I'd be here. Besides, I have something I want to discuss with you; can you see me in a couple of days?"

"I don't think we have anything to say to one another," she replied as coldly as she could manage, given that she felt herself tremble slightly.

"You'd be a fool not to listen to my proposal, Charley, and whatever else you are, you are not a fool." His tone of voice was muted.

He was being reasonable and kind; she was put immediately on her guard. She knew he was a tough negotiator and did not entirely trust him. However, she managed to be neutral when she nodded her agreement, saying: "Thank you for the inverted compliment. We can go into the resident's lounge if you like, or the office. I'd rather we talk now. I might be very busy tomorrow."

"It isn't appropriate now, Charlotte. Make me an appointment, please?"

"I don't want you coming back. I'm busy tomorrow. We do it now or we don't do it at all. It hardly matters anyway."

But he would not be baited. "I want to pitch a deal; now is not the time. You look tired; I would be a heel to have you talk business now."

"If you are worried about being a heel, I have to say it's a bit late for that."

"What do you mean?"

"You know very well." She gave a weak shrug. She was tired; her head hurt; she wanted to curl up in a ball and cry. She looked up at him; he was studying her really hard as if trying to make something out. He was not going to admit what he had done; she did not need him to. However, she relented. Charley was not in the mood for argument or for business. "Can you come the day after tomorrow? The afternoon would suit me best."

"That will be fine. I'll be here at two."

He held out his hand. After a moment's hesitation she took it. He had not lost his firm handshake. "I'll see you then, Charlotte, and do try and rest. You look like you need it."

She wanted to retort, to give him a sarcastic answer, but instead merely inclined her head, then turned and walked away.

~ * ~

"I am impressed," Michael said as they entered the office. Everything was neat and tidy. A computer had been installed and there was an air of efficiency about the office that had not been there on either of his previous visits. She looked better too. In a dark green pants suit, she looked businesslike yet attractive, too. He could see that Charley had dressed with care as if wanting to look as if she truly knew what she was doing.

"I'm so pleased to have your approval," she murmured, managing to convey a good deal of sarcasm in the statement. She perched on the edge of the desk, completely unaware of how provocative the pose was. Michael stood.

She dared a glance. He was *so* attractive, even in a plain navy suit, white silk shirt and red tie. Her mind was threatening to go into overdrive with images of how it had been. Although years had passed, she could still remember vividly the moments when they had been totally absorbed with one another, when they had been tangled together, so close. She had been closer to him than to any human being. Looking at him, older, harder somehow, it seemed impossible that they had ever gone beyond the now, falling into that other world, aware of nothing but the pleasure that cascaded from one to the other. She shuddered and had to bite her bottom lip to stop herself from gasping out loud. Tiny implosions were happening deep inside her, an awakening of the sensuality that had lain dormant all these years. She had to keep in control, not to let her mind dwell on the past.

"What did you want, Michael?" she asked, trying to sound businesslike and abrupt but the words coming out like an accusation.

"To deal," he said smoothly.

"I told you I'm not selling."

"I know you told me that. I don't suffer from memory loss, even if some in this room do."

How wrong. She almost screamed the words at him. *I remember everything and that's the trouble. I remember how you betrayed me, too, only I can't travel that route because if I do,* she thought, *I could hit you with something.* If she let herself go, she could find it in herself to strike out and slap him really hard, as if that would alleviate her pain. Anyway, she was over him now, for goodness sake.. Eight years had gone by, you couldn't carry pain and bitterness for that length of time, not if you were a sane and rational person and she was sane and rational, wasn't she? Actually, right there and then she did not think she could answer the question. She felt she was mad, or certainly close to slipping into a kind of madness.

"Okay," he said, "here's the deal."

She wanted to tell him to just leave; there could never be any deal between them, yet she did not speak. She was not a fool. She knew that he was at the top of the field and you would have to be a raving lunatic not to take some free advice when it was offered. "You want to keep this place and you want to prove you can run it successfully."

"I know that I can," she said.

"And why do you know that?"

She sighed. She owed him no explanation; part of her was demanding that she keep her mouth closed and only speak to ask him to leave, but then another part of her needed to prove something. Needed to let him know she was not the innocent young girl who had worked at the diner, not the girl he would use and then throw away when he was tired of her. She had learned the hard way not to be that girl.

"Because I took a course in hotel management and I have worked in hotels, and latterly in the capacity as assistant manager, so I know the business. Oh, not as good as you do, Michael; I mean no one could be *that* good." She could not resist the sarcasm, although it was wasted on him. He *was* good and knew it. The trade papers talked about him all the time and cited him as an example to anyone who wanted to achieve success. Of course, he had inherited his business. Michael had not had to start at the bottom as she was doing, but he had made a success of it. He had quadrupled the profitability of the chain. He was no one's fool and if, initially, a little nepotism had helped him get his foot on the ladder, he had the ability to stay there because he knew what he was doing and not because he was someone's son. She hated to have to admit that to herself.

"Glad you realise that, Charley, but you can always aim high," his answer was to mock her, albeit lightly. "Okay, but you must admit this place is a dump. It needs a lot of money spent on it. Look, it's fine for commercials but if you want to attract a better crowd then you have to update."

"I know that. But we do good business on dining."

"You can't live on dining, no pun intended. You need to have full rooms every night and you won't get those."

"There isn't a better place in this town. You have to go out of town for something better," she insisted.

"You think?" He was dismissive.

"I know. They commute out to the Swallow or the Midland. But I mean actually in the town itself. There's the Regent, but really? Give me a break. Have you ever stayed there and tried to sleep on those nylon sheets?"

He laughed. "No…"

"And as for their breakfasts, swimming in fat, heart attack morning here we come!"

"With money you could be the best. Without it, at best you're always going to be mediocre. You have to see that, Charley. And when I open a hotel, well…" he shrugged. He saw her blanch, watched the blood run right out of her fine featured face. *Got you*, he thought, and the words did not even, just then, seem unworthy of him.

"You…" she stopped, biting on the word she wanted to use.

"Yeah, it has been said, but my parents were married, so what?" He shrugged nonchalantly. "You should know I don't like to get beaten, Charley."

"You're despicable," she spat.

"Yeah, that too. Heard it, time and time again."

She slid off the desk, standing to face him. It was agony to have to look up at him but she would do it, stare him straight in the face and let him know he might be attempting to beat her, but he would not knock her onto the floor again. He had done that once and it had really hurt, but she had come through. Let him do his worst. He could not do anything else that he had not done, *ever*.

"We'll do it, Michael, we'll get by."

16

"Oh, you will, I'm sure. I think you will do okay at the bottom end of the market. I don't mean that in a derogatory way. There's plenty of room for that kind of place, but I don't think it's exactly what you have in mind, is it?"

She did not answer his question, saying instead, "and where will you build this hotel? Land is in pretty short supply."

"The old Marlborough Mill. "

"Marlborough Mill?" she repeated, thinking of the derelict old cotton mill that had been turned into small units and then finally deserted and laid empty for years.

"Pull it down, build on the land, prime site and you know people just can't wait for me to buy it."

"Then," she asked, "why did you want to buy my dad out if you had the Marlborough Mill site?"

"More cost effective, more central and I liked your dad."

"You were going to buy because you liked my dad. That's hardly the stuff of tough business, is it?" she said, not believing it for one moment.

"No. It wasn't *the* reason, but it came into the equation. Money is the thing that drove the deal. And other things, too. The Marlborough will be a big hotel; I wanted something smaller, more Bijou, than grand plaza. I wanted to do something different."

"Money isn't everything, Michael. I seem to recall you had so little respect for it that you denied having any."

"Hey, slow down there. I never denied having it; I just didn't tell you I had it. Not quite the same thing."

She felt sick... sick and angry and dizzy. She stepped back, resting her hip against the desk, afraid she would do something stupid. She could not wrangle with him like this; it exhausted her, and she did not know how to deal with all these conflicting feelings. He had her on the ropes now. She had to fight back, could not let him see that he had the better of her. If he did, he would go in for the kill. She knew the kind of man he was where business was concerned. He had a hard, tough streak. She almost sighed... and in his private life, too, she recalled, if his treatment of her was anything to go by.

"Listen, Charley, I don't want to do you down, I'm just trying to make a suggestion."

"There's nothing else I want to hear. Don't let your conscience trouble you, Michael. I invited you to get it over with, but now you had better go. Do your worst, I'll survive... somehow."

"Sure you will, Charley; you're a real survivor. I really believe that. I have no doubt you will make something of this place but it won't be what you really want."

"You know what I want, Michael? I want you gone from my life."

"No can do just yet. I haven't told you the deal."

Charley thought him so cool, so sure of himself. He had everything... looks, money, but not, she thought, charity. What was she thinking of trying to cross words with him? He had all the aces up his sleeve.

"I thought your ruining my livelihood was the deal." The words were pathetic; she wanted to call them back and because she could not, tilted her chin and gave him what she hoped was a haughty look.

"Where do you get the idea that I want to ruin you? I have no such idea. I want to give you what you want, honey."

"Don't call me honey."

"I thought you liked it, honey... and I mean liked it a lot."

Her cheeks flushed scarlet. She felt a warm gushing sensation. Even now, after all this time, that dark, rich voice murmuring words in a certain way could make her melt. *Try and get a grip, girl,* she told herself, but knowing it was hopeless. She was feeling so vulnerable; it was the wrong time to go into battle with this man.

"I wish you'd just go," she said helplessly.

"I can help you out; in fact I will help you out."

"Help me out? How?" Curiosity was getting the better of her. Had she finally tipped over into insanity? This man would not do anything to help her out, not unless it meant there was something in it for him. But she had nothing to give him. She looked up at him... he was reading the confusion in her mind, seeing the curious little cat pricking up its ears.

"I can put some money into the hotel, a little here and there to give you a head start... decoration, updating the bathrooms, that kind of thing."

"But that would cost a lot of money; you're not talking about a thousand pounds or so here."

"No, I know that."

Excitement at the prospect was taking over now; with those improvements she knew she could make real headway. He would give her a loan. Fortunately, Charles had owned the property, there was no mortgage, so paying

Michael Hernandez back would be like having a mortgage, which she had been considering, yet he would want something for that. Altruism wasn't *his* middle name.

"You'd want something more than interest?" she suggested. He was studying her carefully, as if giving her an assessment, weighing up her hair, her facial features, his eyes lingering on her mouth, and then downwards looking at her figure. She flushed and flounced away, going behind the desk and sitting on her chair.

"I hope you aren't considering that something else is for sale," she said coldly.

He laughed, but it was not really a pleasant laugh. "Oh no, that's something I never buy, and I am not interested in you in that way, Charlotte. We've been there."

"You're arrogance personified," she snapped. Truth to tell, she had found his perusal of her body faintly arousing. It came from the past she knew that. He had liked to look at her, more than that, he had worshipped her with his eyes. She closed her eyes briefly against the jolt of pleasure that gave her. He was insufferable, hateful, playing games and yet… yet she was letting his sensuality invade her mind, torturing herself with images that were all to do with the past, and had no hope of being experienced again in the future.

"Okay, I'll let you off the hook. I'll arrange this place to have a make-over; you can give me a quarter share in the business in lieu of interest."

"A quarter? Twenty five percent?"

"It was when I did math, something wrong with that?"

Her eyes narrowed; she knew she had to take advice on that. He was a slippery character. It seemed like such a good opportunity, and her first instinct was to grab it with both hands.

"It sounds very good," she was honest enough to admit.

"Yeah, it's a good deal for you, but that isn't all of it. I want something else."

"I thought there'd be a catch."

~ * ~

Charley's mouth opened and closed. She felt she must look like a fish out of water but she was utterly lost for words. She stared at him hard, trying to see beyond the perfect features, to what went on behind his face. He looked so serious, but was he laughing inside? He had thrown her a lifeline and when she gratefully grasped it, he had let it go. How cruel, how totally insensitive! She fought for words but none came. What he had just suggested was preposterous.

"I can see you want to think about it," he said coolly. "But I can only give you two days. I have to be back in the States by Friday."

"Are you crazy?" Words came to her at last. He leaned over the desk, palms flat on the top, elbows bent.

"Maybe I am. Anyone with any sense would see all this as such a hopeless cause, but oddly, to play about with it suits my purpose."

"Play about with it? You're talking about my livelihood," her voice miraculously maintained a level of calm that she was far from feeling.

"Oh no, it need not be that way. You have an alternative. Go ahead and sell to me and get out with a

21

nice amount of money. You could buy yourself a little bed and breakfast somewhere. I'm sure you'll be happy in some rural idyll. Somewhere that doesn't present much of a challenge."

"You know nothing about me. You only think you do."

"I know *all* about you, Charley. I *married* you once, didn't I?"

"And I wonder why you did that?"

"Easy. Because I wanted you in my bed and there was no other way."

She jumped up, raised her hand and knocked one of his arms, sending him off balance. She was satisfied when she saw his hand slide across the desk jerking him forward. Stepping from around the desk, she marched to the door, opened it and stood there.

"I think it's time you left, Mr Hernandez," she said feeling herself in some kind of control.

"Not a problem. The problem is all yours, Miss Bloom."

When he left, she felt her knees start to give way. Somehow she made it out of the office and stumbled to the lift. She took it to the top floor, and then went along the corridor to the door that led into her small apartment. Kicking off her shoes, she went and lay on the bed, waiting for the trembling to subside. Shock, rage, all these things washed over her, leaving her weak and exhausted.

He was, the word came to her, *despicable*, and maybe even that was too weak a description. How could he say that? But maybe it was true? Once she had been in his bed he unceremoniously dumped her, only he did not even have the guts to do the dumping. He let his sister do it for him. His sister and that doe-eyed girl he was engaged to.

Betrothed, that was the word they used, and betrothed for years and years. In their culture, that was as good as being married. Of course, she had been so young, just seventeen and totally naive. She should have given him and all his family a good run for their money; gone to a good lawyer and made all kinds of trouble. Yet being cast aside like that had wounded her too deeply, and it had cut into her pride, too. She caved in and went away. Although half believing it was not true, she had thought he would call her, write to her, even come to see her to explain, to say it was wrong, that he had fixed everything and made it all right. However, he never came and she had never seen him again until last week.

She had the truth now. He had wanted her and a quick marriage was good enough to get her into bed. He had had his fun, and then turned his back on his responsibilities, letting his family tidy up the mess for him. *Spoiled brat*, she thought now, only it was so hard to see him in that light when she imagined him in the distant past. The smiles, the laughs and the silly words they said to each other. It had been so wonderful.

It was late when she pulled herself from the bed, shed herself of her suit and took a shower. She made tea in the small kitchen attached to the living room and as she sipped it she thought about his proposal.

It was a ludicrous idea and she did not even quite believe why he wanted her to do such a thing. But then again, when it came to *dumping* women, he hadn't a very good past record. He had had to get his sister to *dump* her, and Charley had been his wife. If he needed to prove to a woman that he was no longer interested, then surely he did not need her. He could get his sister Maria to do it for him.

"You are my ex-wife," he said, "and if there is one thing guaranteed to frighten off women, it's the reappearance in a man's life of his ex-wife. All that baggage we carry together, good and bad."

"Just tell her it's over," she had argued. "Women do know how to go away, you know."

"This is different. This girl won't go away. She's been hanging onto my coat tails for years, and I've had enough. Besides, nothing is over because nothing ever happened."

"Then get the police involved."

"It's a family thing. I can't do that, Charlotte, really I can't. It sounds weak, I know, but that's how it is."

"I can't play the lovesick ex-wife; it would be far too difficult."

"I'm sure you could, Charlotte, you played it pretty good before."

Her mouth opened and closed. What did he mean? She had not been playing at anything; it was he who played, and then when he had tired of the toy, he had tossed it away.

"Think about it; give me a ring. At least consider it."

~ * ~

The next day, she could concentrate on very little. Michael Hernandez haunted her thoughts. The staff was meeting with her at four and she had to tell them what would be happening.

She had indicated she would carry on because there were bookings to be honoured. So far, she had not heard from the bank on the possibility of a mortgage or a loan and if she planned to re-decorate she would have to close for at least a month. Could she afford to keep the staff on, even the chef, for that length of time with no money coming in and a mortgage to pay? She knew the easiest thing would be to sell; however, she did not like easy. Besides, what would happen to the staff? They had been so loyal to her father, and he had been planning to make sure they had good jobs within the Hernandez group. However, if she went on alone and Michael eventually opened a hotel in the town, then she would always be second best. Should the bank hear that Michael was even considering opening an hotel, they would probably not lend her the money anyway.

They were such good employees; they had stayed with her dad through good times and the recent bad times. They worked hard and she knew the chef could walk in anywhere and get a really good job. He was happy at Blooms, though. He was master of his kitchen and Charles Bloom had never interfered in any way. He was more or less his own boss. She knew, too, that family commitments meant he did not want to move out of town. Yet none of the staff could live off air; they needed to know they would be paid their salaries. Everyone had a mortgage or rent to pay.

Then what would she do? Michael had said, and so contemptuously she really could have slapped him, that she could open a bed and breakfast. He was right. The money he paid for the hotel would enable her to do just that, but she wanted more. A bed and breakfast was fine, but it was not challenging enough for her. Recently she had been an assistant manager at a two hundred and twenty roomed hotel and was used to dealing with a large staff. She was, and she was not being immodest, very good at her job. A small bed and breakfast would not suit at all.

When she saw the staff anxiously gathered, Charley made up her mind there and then. Looking at them all made her realise she had to secure the life of the hotel and their livelihoods, her own career too. It would not be too difficult to go along with Michael; he meant nothing to her... who was she kidding? It would be agony.

"I've had an offer of sorts," she said. "Mr Hernandez has said he will back me to a certain degree."

"He will?"

The murmur went around. She could see this was good news.

"The thing is, I have to go to the States with him, only temporarily, and he would put in a first rate manager."

"Wait a minute, Charley," Chef said. "This bloke isn't going to be dabbling in my kitchen, is he?"

"He'd better not," Charley said. "I am going to make that perfectly clear, Bob. Don't you worry about it."

"If that's so, I'm up for it," he said. "I think we can really go places with a good investment and an upgrade."

She explained there would be a necessity to update; the hotel would be closed but the staff would not be let go. "Call it a paid leave. About two months, but that will start just before I get back, so the hotel will run as normal until then. Is everyone happy about this proposal? There would be an opportunity for some cleaning work, if anyone is interested. I have to discuss terms with Mr Hernandez; if he doesn't agree then I'm not going ahead."

"I'll come in and sort out the kitchen," Chef said. And the chambermaid said she would come in and do cleaning whenever necessary.

Of course they were glad about it. Only Charley was unhappy with the thing she was letting herself in for. After the meeting broke up, she called Michael Hernandez on his cell phone.

"I'll do it," she said. "But I want proper papers drawn up. There are some guarantees that I want."

"Fax your demands today, and then I'll have my lawyer confirm them later."

"Today?"

He grunted; it was almost as if he were trying to hide a laugh. "I had partial papers drawn up just in case. You know me... Boy Scout, always be prepared."

"You knew I'd do it," she accused. "You are such an arrogant..." but she bit on the words.

"No, I didn't know for sure, Charlotte, I just thought you might give it due consideration. If you really want something badly enough, then you make compromises. I learned that very early in my life."

"I'm sure you did, Michael."

Two

In the penthouse apartment in Manhattan, Charley was still wondering what she had let herself in for. She wandered cross the pale cream carpet of the living area going into the kitchen. Coffee had been percolated and, after finding a cup, she poured some in. Drifting out again, she passed by the huge glass doors that let out to a terrace. It was sunny and the light reflected on the tall and elegant buildings of mid-town.

They had arrived yesterday. It was six o'clock New York time but she had gone to bed right away and slept. Not the best of flyers, she always felt a little under the weather after a flight, even one of only seven hours.

A chauffeur had met them and whisked them here in a limousine. Michael had left abruptly, telling her he would see her later. And she had not seen him since.

He had been quiet on the flight, barely speaking but looking out of the plane's window as if, once they were crossing the Atlantic, there was a view. Charley had felt a little strange sitting in first class, being fussed over by a glamorous flight attendant, and indeed one who seemed to know Michael rather well. Without comment, Charley sipped a champagne cocktail as if she were born to it.

Michael ate little and drank one champagne cocktail, then turned to study whatever it was he saw from the window.

She studied him... his perfect profile with that aristocratic Roman nose. His smooth brown skin was freshly shaved; he had to shave twice a day, she remembered that, or his skin visibly darkened with rough beard. She rather liked it when he did not shave. Her toes curled against her leather ankle boots. Those were the kinds of memories she had to stamp on, but it was *so* difficult. His presence had the habit of intoxicating her senses. Charley had to keep reminding herself how he had treated her to stop the thoughts overwhelming her. There was a risk those thoughts could make her do something utterly silly... like touching him.

She liked his hands, the way dark hair very lightly curled at his wrist, after which the skin was pale brown and taut, his fingers long and rather thick. He had strong hands. He could turn his hand to manual tasks without any effort; he worked efficiently and was never clumsy. She had been clumsy when young, had a habit of dropping things, but then she had barely been able to concentrate on doing anything properly when he had been around. *More fool you*, she chided herself.

Now she wandered the apartment, reminding herself she had better not break anything here, for it all looked extremely expensive. How he must have laughed at the domesticity they shared those weeks they were married. They had shared a little snug apartment in New Rochelle.

It had been part of a larger house, not even in an apartment block, but so ideal. She had loved it... the one bedroom, lounge-diner and the little kitchen. It had been wonderful, only a few minutes walk to the beach. However, it had been a dream, just too ideal to be real.

Michael must have laughed about it later, about how he had fooled this girl into believing he loved her, and the way she had thought this dump they rented was so perfect.

She opened doors and peered in; there was a study and library, a den for comfortable relaxing; two bedrooms on one side of the apartment, one of which she had used, and two smaller bedrooms on the other side. He had told her in an off-handed way it was two apartments knocked into one, that's how come it was so huge. The larger bedroom, complete with ensuite bathroom, had the huge glass windows that let out to the terrace. She could imagine it would be spectacular at night, lying in bed with the blinds open, looking at the twinkling lights of the city. The bed was huge, one of those king size canopied beds. There was a beautiful carved desk and matching chair, and a chaise-lounge covered in pale rose silk. She crossed the room and looked in the bathroom. There was a shower, large tub, all pristine white, with large fluffy towels, monogrammed in black MH. Obviously this was Michael's bedroom and she knew she had to get out of there as quickly as possible; one thing she did not want to give him was the wrong idea.

The room she had used was large, too, and it had a shower cubicle, a whirlpool bath and vanity unit. The windows in the bedroom let out to the side of the building, but there was still a terrific view of the city, right along

Fifth Avenue. The chauffeur had left their cases with the doorman downstairs. She thought they might have come up and opened the closet, but it was completely empty. Deciding to telephone the desk and ask whether the concierge had her bags and when would they be arriving, she made to go back into the lounge.

Hearing a door close startled her a little. It seemed rather noisy in the silent stillness of the apartment. It was Michael; he had a bundle of mail in his hand and was flicking through it as he stepped deeper into the apartment. When he had finished, he tossed it onto a marble topped table, then looking up saw her standing by the bedroom door.

"You look like a startled doe," he muttered.

She stepped out, closing the door behind her. He must have been up all night; dark, almost blue stubble stained his complexion. He was wearing a white raincoat; he shrugged out of it and tossed it over a chocolate-coloured leather chair.

"So what do you know?" he asked.

"What could I know? I slept; I just woke up."

"Okay, any coffee?"

She said that there was and he went into the kitchen to help himself. When he came out again, he said. "There is a housekeeper; she doesn't live in, but she comes every day. Her name is Thelma. Anything you want, you ask her. They're pretty good at the desk; they do errands, that kind of thing."

"Eh," she said, trying to be pleasant, which was difficult with all kinds of crazy emotions swarming through her. "This is New York, you send out, right?"

He smiled. "Sure, but you never know, you might want something special." He sipped his coffee, seeming in a thoughtful mood, then seeing her just standing there said. "Make yourself at home; do you want the guided tour?"

"I looked around."

"I arranged for the car to collect you at eleven. Gerry will take you to Bergdorf's. You have an account there and at Bloomingdales and Saks, and anywhere else you want, you let me know. A girl called Carol will be your personal shopper; she will meet you in the lobby. She's going to take you to a couple of designers also"

"Just a moment." Charley put up her hands, "I don't need any clothes; I brought clothes with me and if they aren't good enough…"

"They aren't. Sorry those clothes are out, nice though they were."

"Chain store clothing was good enough for you when we were married," she snapped.

"As I recall," he said softly, "you did not wear very much when we were married."

He smiled when he saw the crimson invade her cheeks, and muttered. "Cool down." When she whispered something unpleasant at him, he merely shrugged. "Can't you take a joke anymore?"

"That wasn't funny," she said, feeling just a little breathless because she remembered the same could be said of him, and a vivid picture of that brown skinned angular body tripped into her mind.

"Maybe not, but it's true."

"I'm going to wear my own clothes," she said, determined not to be defeated by him.

"No can do. I dumped the lot."

"What?"

"Not dumped exactly. I had them sent them to the Thrift Shop."

"How dare you?"

He came towards her; slowly she started to back away... then suddenly stopped. What could he do to her? She had not to let him think that she was afraid of him. He would love that, but the truth to tell, it was not him she was afraid of, it was she and the teaming emotions that cascaded through her when he came close.

"Look, you agreed to this. We do it my way and I want you to wear good clothes and look the part."

"Oh, I'll look the part all right," she returned, narrowing her eyes. "The part of your ex-wife, and one that is so glad that it is ex."

"No, you won't. You will look like you care about me, you will not look like a reluctant bride in any way, because if you do I shall take it you are reneging on the deal, and then I call the whole thing off. You do it properly, Charley, or you don't do it at all."

"I think they call this blackmail."

"No they don't; they call this business." He turned away and went to his briefcase, snapped it open and started pulling out various envelopes. "These are for you... credit cards, and this is your bank account."

"I have my own credit cards and my own bank account?"

"With not much in it, Charley, and I don't want you spending your own money. You're working for me, just take it like that." For a moment, his eyes searched hers

and then abruptly he looked away. "You don't have to
spend a cent if you don't want to, but what if you are
caught out somewhere and need something? It's there for
you.

"Don't be stupid and wilful, Charley, I will take it all
back out of the profit Bloom will make, given time, if it
makes you any happier."

"I have my pride," she said, pushing back her shoulders
and tossing her hair, unaware of how the gesture revealed
the curve of her full high breasts against the softness of
her sweater.

Michael, of course, did not miss it and looked at her.
"Nice," he muttered under his breath.

"What?"

"Nothing. You'd better get ready; it's close on eleven.
Don't worry, Charley, it's only money."

Realising she could do nothing about it, unless she
wanted to wear the sweater and woollen trousers she had
travelled in all day and every day, she made her way into
the second bedroom, and into the bathroom. There were
soaps and towels and she hurriedly washed her face, then
applied a light foundation, combed her well-shaped
eyebrows, then slicked on a deliciously pink lipstick.
Satisfied, she went out to the bedroom, surprised to find
Michael there.

"Did you sleep here?" he asked, indicating the bed. She
had roughly thrown the covers back but had not made up
the bed properly.

"Yes, something wrong?"

"Our room is the bigger one."

"*Our room?* Now wait a minute, Michael, there is no *our* room, I'm not going to sleep with you."

"Yes, you are. We do it properly; the housekeeper would talk if you were in a separate room. I mean sleep; I don't lust after your body anymore. I told you, been there, done that." He spoke matter-of-factly, as if he were merely discussing the weather.

"You really are the pits," she snapped, more hurt than angry. He was so dismissive of her that pain like a knife tore through her. What did she expect? Anyone who could have treated her as he did would not change; at least she should be grateful for his honesty, that way she would never develop any romantic notions that she actually meant something to him.

"I'm not sharing a bed with you to sleep or otherwise, so you can get that straight right now."

"Okay, sleep on the chaise lounge for all I care, but you are not sleeping in this room. This is the room for special guests, and we might be having someone come to stay."

"What kind of someone?"

He did not answer.

She thought of his sister... Maria, the beautiful but spiteful girl whom he had sent to end their marriage. For all her outer toughness, Charley did not think she would be able to deal amiably with that little madam.

"Family," he said, at last confirming her worst fear.

"Do you mean your sister?"

"Which one? One is married and living in Mexico and the other is in college at home."

"I didn't know you had two sisters," she said. "I meant Maria anyway."

35

"Maria? How come you know her name?"

He had the gall to ask the question, obviously pretending he had forgotten she had once been his emissary. The words wanted to spill out of her; the accusations and the anger were all bubbling away on the surface, yet she was exhausted and tired of wrangling with him. The telephone rang out. *Saved,* she thought, *by the bell.*

Michael crossed the room and answered it. It was the chauffeur; he had arrived to collect her.

She took the opportunity to leave without answering his question. He did not really need an answer anyway, because he knew why she knew his sister's name was Maria.

However, at the door she hesitated, had to know for her own peace of mind. "Which sister is in college?"

"My youngest sister, Dolores; she's at college in Florida."

"Florida?"

"That's where I come from; don't tell me I didn't tell you that. God, you must hear it in my accent. Don't tell me I sound like a Yankee."

"No, you don't, and I did know that, I had just forgotten," she lied, for she had forgotten nothing at all about him in those eight years they had been apart.

~ * ~

Everything that she had bought would be delivered, apart from a black silk trouser suit she wanted to take to wear and some lingerie. Carol had looked at her somewhat askance when she had chosen a granny style night dress that buttoned from collar to hem. The personal shopper probably thought that therein lay the reason for Michael's divorcing her, Charley chuckled to herself, when that was so very far from the truth. She recalled the negligee she had bought for their first night together—midnight blue cobwebs of lace that had cost far more than the dress she had worn to their wedding. But it had been so perfect and had been an excellent choice; if she wanted to drive Michael wild, she had only to slip into that negligee and wait for the fireworks. She did not have it anymore; in a fit of heartbroken rage, she had torn it to shreds and put it in the dustbin.

There was one more thing to do before she went back to the apartment. A friendly chat with Carol, the personal shopper, and then a telephone call, had an appointment at a top hairdresser arranged. If there was one thing she knew that Michael was into, it was long hair. It was time to have hers cut. That was a little act of defiance that she felt would give her at least a modicum of pleasure.

"Beautiful hair," the man who was famed for his cutting abilities declared, running his hands through the thick chestnut locks. "And this colour—a real rich brown. You can't buy this colour in a bottle, you know, and you want to *cut* it!"

"Well..." she had asked for an elfin cut, thinking that would be rather fun, only now she felt a trickle of apprehension. Suppose she looked terrible! No woman wanted to look terrible, even one seeking to defy the man who had set himself up as her lord and master.

"Look, how about a compromise? A chin length bob would suit you." He folded up her hair, giving an impression of a chin length style. She had to admit it did look rather nice. "It will be sleek; the colour will be emphasised. Please think about it," he implored gently.

"Okay, do that. I'm scared of looking like a shorn lamb."

"I should think so, too."

When he had finished and she saw her reflection, she was more than pleased. She had, now, with the haircut, an air of sophistication. Her eyes looked larger and more round, her high very fine cheekbones more prominent, and her face— marginally better, she modestly thought.

"I think Mr Hernandez will be more than pleased," the man declared. "You know, I would be frightened that he would come after me if I had shorn all this lovely hair."

"Maybe," she grinned. She had not liked using Michael's name, but it was the only way she could have been sure of getting an appointment. Some things did make life easy, she thought.

"You know, I cut his mother's hair when she is in New York. She is a charming lady."

"We haven't met yet..."

"Be thankful you have kept your hair at least a decent length. She would not have been impressed with a boy's cut, believe me. She is charming but a little old fashioned. You know she came from a very good family in Cuba."

"Oh yes," the white lie slipped easily off her tongue. She had known that the family was of Spanish descent, but she had not known about the Cuba connection. She had assumed they had come from old Spain, and not the new Spain; further, she had not realised they had connections so recent. Michael had seemed so very typically American when they had met, warm, friendly and courteous.

There's a lot I don't know about him, she thought. Perhaps a perusal of his past would give more insight into him, at what made him tick and give reason why his behaviour had been so abominable. But of course, nothing in his past could give an excuse for it, and the sooner she realised that, the better it would be, for herself and for everyone concerned. He did his own thing in his own way and in some ways had to be really unscrupulous. Hardly the kind of person you want for a business partner, let alone a marriage partner, she thought and reminded herself to always remember that fact.

~ * ~

"What the hell have you done to your hair?" he demanded, as she came in the door and before she could put down her parcel or shrug out of her leather jacket.

"Had it cut, I mean that's what we call it."

"Why in all that is holy, have you cut your beautiful hair?"

He appeared so angry, storming across to her side, seizing hold of her arm and twirling her around as if he could not quite believe it was not pinned up at the back. She was, seeing his reaction, a little disappointed she had not gone the whole way and really created a shocking new image!

"You seem to forget, I'm independent of you," she retorted, "and I can do as I like. I don't have to get your permission to have my hair cut. You're behaving like some medieval patriarch!"

" If you want to look a mess, that's your problem, but it's only your problem after the deal is finished. I was going to take you out to dinner, but now…"

"Surprise for you, Michael, I don't want to go out to dinner with you."

"But you will be out to dinner with me, providing you have something decent to wear." Michael was staring at her, seeming to probe deep inside her, as if it were possible for him to read beyond her attitude, to what lay beneath the surface.

Afraid, she turned away from his gaze.

"I have," she said, sweeping past him. "And the rest of the stuff will arrive shortly. Would you like to dress me, Milord? I only await your pleasure."

"My pleasure? My pleasure would be to…" He bit on whatever he was going to say, only adding in a voice dripping with sarcasm, "and thanks for the invite, I might just do that. Glad to hear you're getting to know your place."

"Oh, you're so impossible," she said, going into the bedroom and catching onto the door before it slammed. He *was* impossible. Always had something to say just when she thought her own sarcasm had come to her rescue.

After carefully locking the bathroom door, she filled the tub and poured in some heavenly scented bath foam; it was great to relax and ease her tired bones. She still felt ever so slightly jet lagged and felt herself falling asleep in the tub. Hurriedly she left it and after towelling herself dry, wrapped a huge bath sheet around her, went into the bedroom and climbed onto the bed. She just slid under the emerald satin eiderdown and no sooner was her head on the pillow than she fell fast asleep.

It was dark; the lights of the city were twinkling at the windows in other buildings; there was a soft glow from a lamp. Turning away from the huge window, she saw a sliver of light showing beneath the bathroom door. There was the sound of movement so she knew that Michael was in there. Across the room, draped on the chaise, were packages. As quietly as she could, she crossed the room. The package containing lingerie was there. She pulled out a black satin teddy, then the Victorian night dress that she went and tucked beneath the pillow she had used, smiling as she did so. Someone would be in for a shock and it would not be her!

Quickly, she found the body lotion she had bought, put some on her palm and carefully rubbed it over her shoulders and then down her legs. Sliding into the teddy, she let the towel fall, before crossing to where she had hung the black silk trouser suit, together with its matching high heeled, thin strapped shoes.

There was a huge chervil mirror; seeing her reflection gave her a pleasant surprise. The chin length bob really suited her, and as the hair stylist had said, seemed to emphasise the richly chestnut colour of her hair. It was hard not to stare; she had never had her hair so short or in such a stylish cut. So entranced was she with this new image that she did not hear the bathroom door opening. The first she realised Michael was in the room was when his reflection loomed up in the mirror behind her. He was bare to the waist, a towel tied around his middle.

Dizzily she stared at him, at his broad shoulders and firm chest, the slight rough dark hair that spiralled down to his navel in a thin, perfect arrow-shaped line. The image momentarily paralysed her, so much so she forgot she was standing there in a sleekly fitting teddy that emphasised the thrust of her breasts and curve of her hips, against the narrowness of her waist. When feeling came back to her, it was in each of her erogenous zones, tightening her flat nipples until they felt sore, and as tight and thrusting as arrow heads. The bud of her womanhood throbbed and seemed to part itself moistly against the thin silk that rested against it. She almost gasped with the pain of it.

She started to do battle with this tide of sensuality when Michael seized hold of her and turned her around roughly, wrapping her in his arms none too gently, and placing his lips over hers. She attempted for a mad moment to keep her teeth firmly clenched but she could sense the taste of him; that warm intoxicating scent that made denial impossible. Slowly she relaxed her lips, letting him part them, feeling the stampeding emotion rising up inside her, as he plundered the inside of her mouth.

His hands were all over her, down her back, sliding against the silky undergarment she wore, finding it easy to slide his hand inside and moving very gently, caressing the soft flesh of her hip.

Involuntary her legs parted, feeling him aroused through the thickness of the towel. She moved herself against his hard masculinity, knowing she was spinning out of control, that her brain was no longer counselling caution, that it was her body's needs that had total control. Her hands slid down him, against the hard flesh of his back, her eager fingers imploring him to move close, so close there would be no space between them.

The thin silken straps holding her flimsy garment together slid from her shoulders, manipulated down her arms. His hands found her breasts; the pink centres sore with yearning sprang to life at his touch. Charley cried out when his mouth slid from hers, to slide down, his tongue circling the rosy tips, his mouth taking one and then other into the warm moist inside. Every part of her throbbed with need; she arched herself against him, willing him to overpower her, to make her his. Suddenly, when she thought that he could no longer resist, he let her go, breaking free from her clasp, stepping away from her and tightening the towel at his waist.

He said nothing, but padded across the carpet, slamming the bathroom door closed behind him. Weakly, she moved towards the chaise lounge, sank onto it and waited for the trembling to subside. She ached with longing for him, waited for it to pass, closed her eyes against the sensual rhythmic beat of her body. She heard the shower running and then the clatter of things once it stopped. She thought she heard a fist smash against something but could not be certain.

Swiftly moving, she slid into the silk pants suit; going to the dressing table and slicking on some makeup, her hands still so unsteady she could not trust herself to put on some lipstick. She threw the lipstick and small mirror into her bag. She would have to colour her lips later. Her hands were trembling. Nervously she went out into the lounge.

There was a bottle of wine chilling in a silver bucket. Its top had been loosed and she took up a glass and poured a little wine into it, then went and sat in the huge armchair that faced the terrace doors.

Sipping the wine, she stared out at the twinkling windows of other skyscrapers, trying to calm herself and wondering how she had let herself get into such a situation. He had ended it; thank goodness he had, she thought, it had been agony to have her passion turned off so suddenly, yet it would have been even more agonising had they made love.

She did not want that, swore never to go down that road again with him of all people, the husband who had so unceremoniously walked out on her. How could she be so stupid, she castigated herself, knowing the weakness was despicable, yet it would always be there. No matter what he had done, how he had hurt her, there was something he exuded that awakened in her mind and in her body, a potent desire. She gave it a name. *Sex. Pure and simple.* She was not going to wrap it up in any fancy euphemisms. It was purely physical and perfectly understandable, for whatever else he had not liked about her, he had certainly enjoyed her *that* way. The last time they had been together, two days before Maria appeared on the scene, they had made love passionately. There was nothing in that lovemaking that had warned her he was tiring of her; it was easy to see why. The old three letter word again. *Sex.*

She heard the door opening and dared herself to turn around. Michael was dressed in a dark navy suit, white shirt and plain silk tie. He looked immaculate and in control. He said nothing but went and poured himself a glass of wine then asked if she wanted some. She said she had had a glass but perhaps a drop more? He half filled her glass, then put the bottle back into the bucket before going and sitting on the settee just to the right of her.

His voice was vaguely husky about the edges when he spoke. "Sorry about earlier. I didn't intend to do something like that."

She wanted to say... *why did you?* Yet she said nothing. Better not to retaliate than start a cross examination on her ability to still turn him on after all these years.

"Sexy lingerie," he muttered. "It'll do it every time."

"I'm afraid I don't know about that," she said primly. "But perhaps now you will see how sensible it will be to have separate rooms."

"I can see that," he said. "If anyone had told me I'd ever be turned on by you again, I'd have had them incarcerated."

"Thank you for that." The nerve of the man! Anyone would think she had dumped him.

"Think nothing of it. This dinner tonight, please don't mistake my being attentive to what went before."

"Why would you be attentive?" she asked.

"Because we are dining with family friends. Okay, let's go if you're ready. Do you mind walking? I have a feeling I need the air and its only four blocks."

"That sounds good," she answered.

"Get your coat, Charley. I know it's only October but sometimes it can get real chilly at night."

She had purchased a cream cashmere jacket with a mandarin collar. He raised an eyebrow when she came from the bedroom but whether it was approval or not she was not sure, and she certainly was not inclined to ask.

They walked downtown close but not touching hands, nor did she link her arm through his. It was a beautiful night; there was the faintest of breezes but it was not that cold. She remembered other times they had been in New York… they had stayed for two nights in what she thought was a fancy hotel, but which he probably considered down market. They walked in Central Park and ate in simple Italian restaurants, and then by mutual consent headed back to their room. She wondered if *he* ever thought about it… his grand deception… she almost smiled but felt too bitter to give into whimsy.

It was one of those small, intimate chic restaurants, probably only known to locals. The proprietor greeted Michael as if he knew him really well and said their guests had arrived and were already seated at the table. "Your favourite table, Mr Hernandez," the man said.

It was not too dim in the restaurant; there was subtle lighting and candles. The man led them to a table at the far end of the room. It was circular, the white cloth sparkling; there were tiny flowers, gleaming silver cutlery, heavy damask napkins. A man older than Michael stood, then his companion, a small younger woman. She had lots of hair, wrapped high around her head in glowing coils. She was exquisitely formed, tiny and perfect and very,

very, Charley noticed with sinking heart, beautiful *and* familiar.

"Darling," Michael said and for a moment she thought he was speaking to the little woman, but his arm slid around her own waist and she realised it was she who was his darling, at least for now. "I would like you to meet our family's oldest friend, Jose Mendoza and this is his daughter, Mercedes. Jose, Mercedes, this is Charlotte or as she now likes to be known, Charley, my wife."

The girl smiled coolly, extended her hand, then the man did the same. Sliding up to Michael she stood on tiptoe and kissed his cheek.

"Now, Michael, you forget, Charley is your ex-wife," she said sweetly and without venom.

But there was venom there, Charley knew it. She knew Mercedes, too, for it was she who had come with Maria to tell her Michael had finished with her, that he was going to marry Mercedes, that Mercedes was his *betrothed.*

Charley felt like someone had kicked her in the stomach. Something welled up inside her. *I can't do this,* she thought, dine with this woman. And the word, one she hated but felt appropriate, tripped into her mind, this little *bitch!*

What in all that was holy was going on? This was the girl he had left her for, the one he was supposed to be going to marry. Eight years had gone by and he still had not married her. The thoughts tossing around in her head were making her dizzy. She excused herself and headed for the ladies room.

It was cool in there; she rested her face against the cool clean tile. Her heart was hammering away as if she had run twenty blocks. Charley could not go through with this… had to get out of the restaurant. She desperately wanted to go home, not the apartment but over the Atlantic, back to her home town where she had carved out a life for herself. Going to the sink, she dampened a handkerchief and held it to her cheek, first one then the other, then ran it across her brow, disturbing the perfect symmetry of her fringe. What was he up to? Oh for sure, he was up to something, playing some kind of vicious game for his own ends.

Curious as ever, she knew she had to find out. That she would not just throw everything away, she was not afraid, was she? *Of Mercedes Mendoza? No way.* The spiteful miniature Venus might have frightened her once, when she was young and naïve, and the two women, older and craftier, had taken advantage of her. She had not known how to fight then, but she did now. She was a woman and Michael still might be able to arouse her but other things had changed. She had changed. The Mercedes Mendozas of the world no longer intimidated her. The pampered princess was in for a shock if she thought she could do that any more.

Michael and Jose stood as she rejoined their table. Mercedes had manoeuvred herself next to Michael; the only vacant place was across from him. She headed there but Michael caught her arm. "Jose will change places. I want Charley close to me, and I don't want her to escape, again…"

Charley shot a glance at him before looking at Mercedes; the woman's eyes narrowed for a moment, but it was too quick for the men to notice. Charley smiled at her, then she took the seat Jose had vacated and sat next to Michael.

As she settled herself, she felt his hand on her knee; he very gently squeezed the knee cap, then slid his hand away. Was it a warning, or a signal that she was doing all right? The waiter handed out the menus; she handed hers back.

"Michael, you order for me, you know what I like," she smiled up at him.

"I would never trust a man to order for me," Mercedes said in her whisper soft little girl voice. "They always order far too much, and I like to take care of my figure. If I even reached size eight, I would have to go on a diet. You obviously do not diet, Charley."

How patently obvious you are, Charley thought, *and childish to boot. You don't really know how to play the game, Mercedes, I am older and smarter than I was and I know so much more than I did then.*

"She's forbidden to diet," Michael said.

Jose coughed and then launched into general conversation; it was a relief to be able to listen and to add something without having to be on her guard. Yet her mind drifted, travelling back over the years, remembering the two women and their assured attitude. *They had lied!* She saw it now quite plainly. If Michael had wanted to marry Mercedes, he would have done so by now. However, even if they had lied she did not think they had done it of their own accord. Michael was behind it and now, for some reason, he wanted to pretend to Mercedes that he was getting back with Charley. It was easy to understand why. She was the one who was clinging. This was the woman he wanted frightened off. As he had once wanted to get rid of her, Charley, he now wanted to get rid of Mercedes.

What had he said? She would not take no for an answer, so it was not a question of him telling her. He had to go further than that because unlike her, Mercedes Mendoza was incapable of going quietly. She was a clinging vine, and he wanted her cut away from him once and for all.

Really, he should marry Mercedes; they were so alike thought Charley. *Spoilt and using any one in any way to get what they wanted.*

It was tempting to think of causing a scene, ending it with Michael there and then and letting him fight off Mercedes in any way he could, but she had struck a deal with him. Besides, she owed Mercedes some pay back. She would really enjoy that.

Slowly and with purpose and not pausing in appearing interested in the conversation, she placed her hand on top of Michael's. He immediately clasped her hand, enveloping it in his own warm dry palm, running a finger along her fingers with loving care as if she were so very precious to him.

The food was delicious. Charley tried to do justice to it, but her mind was still spinning out of control. Besides, she had to concentrate on replying to Mercedes' sly little barbs which continued to be hurtled across the table. In a last attempt to exclude Charley from the conversation, Mercedes began talking about their youth. The times they spent together, the things they did; high school stuff about proms and football games and so much fun. It seemed to

Charley that they appeared to have such a good time that no academic work was ever done, yet that could not be true for Michael was intelligent and well educated, so he must have done plenty of work.

"It was always the three of us—the three Ms, everyone called us—Miguel, Maria and Mercedes."

"And who is Miguel?" Charley asked.

Mercedes sniffed. "Why, Michael, of course, he was Miguel. Then he went all Anglo on us. He is still Miguel to his mother, is that not so, Miguel?"

"When she is speaking Spanish. If she's speaking English, even she calls me Michael," he said lightly.

"Why did you change it?" Charley asked.

"Why did you become Charley?" he snapped back; the irritation in his voice was not overlooked by either Jose or Mercedes. Charley saw them exchange a meaningful glance. They both suspected that all was not quite as it seemed.

"Sorry," Michael said suddenly. "Didn't mean to snap at you, honey, but all our yesterday's garbage wears me down."

"Michael, how rude," Mercedes said. "You know we shared some really happy times." Her jet black eyes grew wide and soft; she looked at him in a hurt way.

"Of course we did," he said. "But it was years ago and you have to go on with your life. We had a great time growing up, but it's gone now. Wasn't it Gatsby who said you can't repeat the past?"

"It was actually Nick Carraway," Charley said. "But you have the right novel."

"There you go, my little expert on American literature. More wine anyone?" his smile encompassed them all.

~ * ~

It was a relief when it was over. The other two took a cab, and Michael and Charley walked back to the apartment. A chilly wind had got up and she was glad of the cashmere jacket.

"Is Mercedes the pursuer?" she asked.

"Yes. She's a good girl, but she's like a kid sister. I could never see her as she would like to be seen."

"She might be just what you need," Charley suggested, although she meant it sarcastically. *The two would go well together; they could talk about their golden youth when things got a little boring,* she thought with unusual maliciousness.

"Believe me, she isn't. I don't intend to make the mistake of marrying any woman again."

"You learned your mistake very quickly," she said.

"I sure did," he said darkly.

The warmth of the building wrapped itself around them as they went inside. The elevator silently transported them up to the penthouse. She thought to say something about the visit of Mercedes and Maria, but she felt too tired to argue. It would cause a terrible row. She would have to let out all those feelings she kept hidden. Now was not the time; perhaps in the cold light of day she would say something, let him know how despicably he had behaved, for he did not seem to understand he had done anything wrong. The way he acted anyone would have thought she had done the dumping.

Once in the apartment, she went into the second bedroom, took off her clothes and went into the shower after locking the door. She took a lukewarm shower and then slipped into the Victorian night dress. When she was ready, she unlocked the bathroom door, going into the bedroom. The light had been turned off; the blinds were down and it was pitch black in the room. She stumbled around, trying to feel for a light switch and ended up banging into a piece of furniture. With reluctance, she called out. "Michael, I can't see a thing in here."

The light switch clicked and the room was flooded with light; it was not the dressing table she had banged into but the open closet door.

"What are you doing?"

"You turned off the light," she accused.

"I didn't know you were coming in here."

"This is where I'm sleeping," she protested.

"You are not. I told you, we sleep in the main bedroom. We might have visitors any day soon."

"There are the spare rooms."

He raised his eyes to heaven. "Charley, I told you." His voice was clipped, his eyes, surprisingly for such dark brown eyes, were quite cold. "You stay in my room, in my bed. That's the way things are done, and that's the way you'll do it."

"And I told you," she snapped right back. "After tonight's episode…"

He leaned against the door, arms folded and a twisted smile at his mouth. "You don't imagine that getup is going to turn me on, do you? You have a high opinion of yourself if you do. You look like Little Red Riding Hood's Grandma."

"Michael, I'm very tired, I don't want to argue. Tonight was a real strain."

"Charley, you made a deal. It was a strain for me, too. I'm tired, too, so let's go to bed and get some sleep. I haven't slept since we got here, and I have a real busy schedule tomorrow."

"That's hardly my fault."

"I never said it was. Charley, just get to bed and cut out this arguing."

She looked at the bed. What would he do if she just went and got in and pulled the cover over her head? Surely he would not drag her out of it. She glanced at him.

"Don't even think about it," he said as if he read her mind.

"You…" It was the politest thing she could think to say. She crossed to where he was, slid past him and went into the lounge and through the other door into the master bedroom. Even before he arrived, she was in the bed at the very far side of it.

She heard the rustle of the sheets; the light switched off. She lay in the darkness very tensely for about fifteen minutes until the steady breathing of Michael told her he was already asleep. She relaxed her legs, uncurling her tense toes and very soon she, too, fell asleep.

A noise disturbed her; she opened her eyes. There was a faint glimmer of light coming through the partly opened blinds. Slowly she turned in the bed, trying not to make any noise. The other side of the bed was empty. Across the room she saw Michael. He was wearing pale blue silk pyjama bottoms and he was, as quietly as possible, taking out of the closet a shirt and dark suit, before he crossed the carpet very softly and slid into the bathroom closing the door quietly. In moments she heard the sound of the shower running.

She slid her arm across the bed, but could not reach where his body had been. She rolled herself closer until her head touched his pillow, and her body slid onto the warm sheet where he had lain. She could smell his familiar scent; it tickled her senses, the familiar intoxication rushed over her. She closed her eyes against the hypnotising effect and very soon fell into a second and more contented sleep.

Charley awakened again, only this time she could smell the aroma of fresh coffee percolating. A knock sounded on the door just as she was about to leave the bed. Nervously she called, "Come in."

It was a woman, round and smiling and of late middle age. "Hi, Ma'am, I'm Thelma. Would you like some coffee?"

"Hello, Thelma. I certainly would."

In moments the woman was back with a tray, coffee pot, cup, and cream and sugar bowl.

"This is style," Charley said brightly. "My dreams come true."

"Not a problem," Thelma said. "Mr Hernandez said to wake you around ten if you weren't about."

"Gosh, is it turned ten?" She glanced at the clock.

"Not quite."

"I must try and get up earlier, Thelma; I'm really a lark."

"Sorry, Ma'am?"

"I like to be up early, early to bed, that kind of person. I am not one of those night owls."

"You're like Mr Hernandez then," Thelma said. "Now, Ma'am, what would you like for breakfast?"

"Just cereal and toast, nothing special, thank you, Thelma."

Of course Michael was like her, she remembered only too well. Early to bed and early to rise, only bed had not been a place to have much sleep in those early days of their brief but ecstatically happy marriage.

After drinking a cup of coffee, she went into the bathroom and took a shower, disturbed by the thoughts that would not leave her alone. Last evening Michael had quoted from *The Great Gatsby* to say you could not relive the past, and here she was doing just that in her mind. How was it possible Michael had just decided so suddenly he did not love her anymore? Had it really been just about sex. Had there never been a moment when it had been more than that?

How did she know anyway? She had had no experience of men before Michael and precious little after. He would be surprised, she knew, to know she had not shared a bed with any other man since their marriage had ended. Once bitten had been a mantra for her. Any man who had aspirations had been frozen out by her glacial attitude. It had been so easy to be glacial, too, for the pain could all too easily be recalled into being whenever she felt like it.

Amongst the things she had bought had been a couple of track suits. She slipped into one and decided to go down to the gym Michael had told her was on the ground floor of the apartment building. One thing she knew for sure… a good old fashioned workout would drive out these debilitating thoughts.

By the time she arrived back, Thelma had gone food shopping, after ascertaining what was needed. Charley would have liked to have gone with her and said she would the next time Thelma would be going. "I know you can get everything online, but I do like trawling round a supermarket now and again," she said.

"Me too," Thelma admitted, "I like to see what different kinds of things they have. I'll take you next week; you will be here next week, Ma'am?"

"It seems like it," she admitted. After all, Michael had said it would be a two month assignment and although she had thought of just walking away, she knew she could not really do that. It would not be possible to let her people at the hotel down. She had made promises, and she had to see them through. It was these promises, and not the promises she had made to Michael that kept her onboard. After all, he was not very good at keeping promises himself.

Thelma had left a salad for lunch. After a quick shower, she changed into a pair of well cut jeans and a lightweight bright red sweater. She ate the salad sitting at the breakfast bar, and took a glass of water with it. The afternoon stretched before her and she thought she might go and tour New York. She knew the city; on her days off when she had worked outside the city, she had come in to explore.

The man her mother had married had been an American. They had gone to live in a small town in

Connecticut and, before deciding what she wanted to do with her life, Charley had come over with them. She found temporary work at various places. Everything about her life seemed temporary just then. Her mother was settled and happy with her new husband and when he had a job transfer offered in Arizona, they had gone there. She had not wanted to go so far and she had stayed behind; found a room to rent and took the job at the diner while she made up her mind what she would do. Her mother had not minded, in fact neither of them had, they were so wrapped up in each other, and there was little time for Charley.

It was odd that her mother had fought so hard for her when her marriage broke up, and then made it difficult for her dad to see her. When she met Brad, everything else was let go. Still, Charley had not been bitter. She had been only too pleased to know her mother had found someone to love again after years of being alone. Resentment would have seemed to be a very mean-spirited emotion.

When she heard the door open, Charley turned, expecting to see Thelma with the shopping and ready to leave the chair to help her. She was stopped in the movement. It was not Thelma. It was a small elegant woman with grey hair that had a blue hue to it, but without being artificial. The hair was long and swept up in an elegant chignon. Her vivid dark eyes swept Charley rather arrogantly. There seemed to be a question on her lips, but then she merely asked.

"Are you Charlotte?"

There was a faint accent and a degree of hauteur Charley found rather intimidating.

"Yes…" Charley stood, nervously pushing her hands into the pockets of her jeans. The older woman saw her and gave her a disparaging look.

"I'm Michael's mother, Yolanda Hernandez."

"Oh, I should have guessed!" Charley said.

"Oh, really?" Mrs Hernandez said rather coldly.

"You look a little like him… the eyes…"

This is not the way to treat a mother-in-law, Charley thought; *I am not making a good impression*, completely forgetting for the moment that Mrs Hernandez was not her mother-in-law and that she did not have to impress anyone.

"Michael told me you were here. Herbert is bringing up my bags. I'm here for two days," the woman said. "I will just go to my room… tea would be pleasant."

"Fine, I'll make some."

Mrs Hernandez swept into the second bedroom. Charley saw then why it was Michael had insisted she not sleep there. Mrs Hernandez had referred to it as *her* room, yet there were no personal items to suggest it really was hers. It was as impersonal as a room in a hotel.

As she made the tea, Herbert the doorman arrived with two medium suitcases. He said he would take them through for Ma'am and knew exactly where to go, further confirming that Mrs Hernandez always used that room. Herbert was not long and came from the bedroom pocketing a tip with a broad smile. Obviously, Mrs Hernandez was popular.

The tea made in a china tea pot, Charley set out a cup and saucer and found the milk, sugar and sweeteners, in case Mrs Hernandez preferred those. Thinking of the elegance of the woman, she could not visualise her perching at the breakfast bar, so set the tea things on the coffee table in the seating area.

Michael's mother appeared after about five minutes, still wearing the elegant dark brown suit with the fitted jacket that emphasised the smallness of her waist. Charley gauged the woman to be about just turned sixty. She was very elegant still and quite beautiful in a rather cold way. There was an aristocratic haughtiness about her. Charley could see where Michael got his good looks, as along with the arrogance he now and again displayed if things were not going his way.

"So we meet at last," Mrs Hernandez said, settling herself on the settee. "Come and sit here, Charlotte."

It was a command not a request and though it irked to be spoken to as if she were a maid here for an interview, Charley nonetheless ambled across the floor and went to sit in the chair indicated by Yolanda Hernandez.

"What is going on?" Michael's mother asked very directly.

"I'm sorry?" Charley feigned ignorance.

"Don't be naïve, Charlotte, it ill becomes you. What is going on with you and Michael? How come after all this time you have decided to fall in love again?"

"The heart has its reasons," Charley said lightly, remembering the title of a book and at once regretted her flippancy.

Mrs Hernandez was not amused and said. "That is ridiculous."

"Is it? Is it really ridiculous that I could love Michael?"

"Of course not," she said bristling with motherly pride. "But I just wonder why he has suddenly discovered that he loves you."

Charley winced, *that really hurt.* As a put you in your place statement, it was arrogant as well as hurtful. Did this woman really mean she considered her, Charlotte Bloom, not to be good enough for her son? Financially they were not equal but in every other way they were.

"I see that you appreciate that."

"I don't actually. I am just as good as your son, Mrs Hernandez. He is no better than I, and I am no better than he."

"No, I don't suppose you are, but that was not quite what I meant, Charlotte."

"I call myself Charley now."

Mrs Hernandez shuddered. "I do so hate girls who give themselves boys' names; I cannot see the point of it. Besides, Charlotte is such a beautiful name."

"Maybe, but I rather like Charley. It brings me closer to my dad."

"Ah yes, your father. You recently lost your father, Charlotte, and I am sorry for that."

"Thank you. It was hard to lose him when I'd only recently found him again. It was one of life's cruel jests."

"It can seem that way, but I think everything happens for a reason."

Yolanda Hernandez poured her tea and took it black. She lifted the cup and saucer and held it elegantly; in fact everything she did was elegant and stylish. Her hands were small yet with long thin fingers, the nails not too talon-like but just long enough and coloured bright red.

Her legs were held together, as were her feet. They were shod in brown leather high heeled court shoes; a woman, Charley saw, of great poise and felt a lump by comparison.

"So your eyes met across the proverbial and you realised you could not live without one another. How romantic."

Charley laughed; she was not certain whether Mrs Hernandez was being serious or not but the image was quite funny.

"Hardly that way," Charley said.

"I don't believe it. However, if you want to play along with this game of charades, then do so."

"Why don't you believe it?"

"I have my reasons, and they are much truer than those of the heart," she said. "Anyway, it is his business. I know he does not want to marry Mercedes Mendoza, that he never has, but he does not wish to hurt her because they have always been friends. Our two families have been very close for many years."

Some friend, Charley thought, but she bit back on the words.

"I wouldn't know about that," she murmured.

"But you, Charlotte, you will do something for me."

"I will?" Charley swallowed a little. The intensity of the woman's gaze was disturbing. She was in some ways glad that Michael's mother was not entirely fooled by his machinations because she did not enjoy telling lies, especially not to someone as close to Michael as his mother. She was no deceiver; with Mercedes Mendoza, she could not really care less, that was an entirely different matter. However, she could not admit to his mother that she and Michael had struck a deal. She might be uncomfortable with the lie but it was up to Michael to confirm or deny the truth of it.

"I know what happened eight years ago."

Charley gulped a little; she felt her heart start to accelerate.

"And what was that?" she asked, though she did not really need confirmation. There were only two things that happened eight years ago. One was her marriage to Michael and the other was his sending his sister and their friend to tell her it was over. They told her it was a not a proper marriage anyway because it had not been in a church. Charley had checked later and found the marriage was legal in law and that was all that had mattered to her at that time.

"They should not have done that," Mrs Hernandez said. "It was unforgivable, although it was done for the best of motives."

"Mrs Hernandez, I don't understand."

"No, I don't suppose you do. Michael, you see, did not send his sister and Mercedes to you. They came of their own volition."

Three

It was a form of cowardice, she knew, but reeling from what Yolanda Hernandez had told her, Charley had to find a place to be alone. The opportunity for her to leave came when Thelma came back. The woman greeted Mrs Hernandez warmly but was ordered immediately to go and unpack Mrs Hernandez's suitcase.

It was the opportunity Charley needed. "Please excuse me, Mrs Hernandez. I have something to do."

"Of course," the woman said, as if completely unaware of how mortified Charley was by her cold disclosure of the truth. "You will think about what I asked?" she added in a casual way, as if she had not really meant the request.

"You can rely on me," Charley said. "I just want to forget the whole thing."

Charley left the lounge, and after reaching her bedroom, she managed to close the door softly. She pulled off her clothes and climbed onto the bed, then burrowed like a wounded animal beneath the eiderdown. She pulled it over her head, blocking out the light, stuffing it into her mouth so that her heaving sobs could not be heard.

She tried to tell herself it did not matter now. The years had gone by but they had not eased her pain any. He had, she thought, broken her heart and ruined her for anyone else. She mentally accused him of making it so she could never ever trust another man. Now she discovered he had done nothing of the kind.

It had all been lies thought up by his sister and her best friend. They had taken such a terrific gamble, but she had believed them. She never gave Michael a chance. Never contacted him to confirm what she had been told. How convincing they had been and how vulnerable and low on self esteem she had been at that time.

She had never been able to quite believe that Michael … handsome, wonderful Michael… could really love her. She imagined she was nothing in comparison to him. It was easy to believe he had left her and yet the truth was, he had not ruined her life, other people had done that and she had let them. In a way he had let them, too, for what had they told him? And why had he believed it so much that he had never tried to find her? He never came to ask her what had happened. Perhaps in part they had been so confident their plot would work because they knew he did not love his new wife quite as deeply as he should. Perhaps when he had been home, he had let something slip and that had given them the incentive to carry out their despicable plan.

She thought, I hate them, all of them and Yolanda Hernandez too, for what she asked for. Charley's silence.

"You must promise me you will not tell Michael," the woman had requested coldly and she had not implored, she had almost demanded Charley to keep her silence.

"Not tell him?" she had cried out in desperation. "How can you expect me not to tell him? Why should I let him believe I'm the kind of girl that just runs off and leaves a man without any explanation? He had to have felt some hurt?"

Mrs Hernandez's eyes narrowed, but she said nothing about whether her son was hurt or not.

"The point is that it is all in the long ago past. If you tell him, it could cause a rift in our family, and believe me, Charlotte, family is all important to me. It is what keeps me going. My family. I never want them to be at odds with one another. They must always be together in friendship and in love. Maria was very wrong, and I do not expect you to forgive her, but she was acting out of the best of motives."

"The best of motives? How is that? She made her brother unhappy!"

"For a time but, Charlotte, you have to see it would never have worked. You and Michael are two very different people. You are right to say he is not better than you, and vice-versa, but my dear, he is different. Your backgrounds are different, your ideals. We are a close knit family. We are Spanish; we adhere to a culture very different from yours."

"Michael seems like the all-American man to me," she said tartly.

"What he seems and what he is are two very different things. Of course he is an American, but he adheres to his Spanish culture, too. It is an adherence for right or wrong that his father and I have always encouraged. Of course, you can play your little game with him now, for whatever reason, but then you will go away, Charlotte. He will expect you to do that. He will not want you in his life permanently. He wants you to be with him, for whatever reason he has, and then you will part, sometime. I do assure you, Charlotte, there will be absolutely no going back to how it was eight years ago. I don't want you to be hurt, Charlotte, but I do assure you, that is the truth. You must not entertain romantic notions about Michael. He would never marry you again."

She looked at Yolanda Hernandez. Her eyes were not like Michael's at all. They were hard, really hard, and she had always thought that hardness in brown eyes was impossible.

"Because of what he believes I did to him," she said, and she felt that nip of pain that never had left her.

"I will be honest, that has much to do with it. But he is over that now. He knows it would never work between you, that it was all wrong in the first place. I have heard him say that. He was glad it ended when he looked at it rationally. You must believe me, Charlotte; he knows that now and has done so for a very long time."

"I thought I was over him, too," Charley lied in part, for she would give this woman no advantage over her. "I'll think about it," she said. Then Thelma breezed in much to Yolanda Hernandez's chagrin.

The eiderdown muffled every sound and buried beneath it she was even unaware of it growing dark. The first she knew of anything, or anyone, was when she felt a hand placed on her shoulder. She started up, tumbling up out of her burrow.

"What are you doing?" Michael was looking down at her. Conscious of her stuffed nose and perhaps a puckering of the flesh beneath her eyes from her tears, she turned away from him.

"I've a cold," she lied.

"Yes, Mom said you were not feeling too good."

Mom, how American was that, she thought. Yolanda Hernandez should be Mamma, or some such equivalent in Spanish.

"So, don't catch it," she said.

"I won't. Will you stay in bed or just 'til dinner?"

He was walking away. She murmured that she would stay in bed, the better to rid herself of the bug and not spread it around.

He made no demur, so she pulled the eiderdown over her head once more. The next thing she was aware of was the eiderdown being tugged a little. She pushed it down and saw that Michael had joined her and was closer to her side of the huge bed than his own.

"What are you doing?"

"Resting," he said. He raised a hand and put it against her forehead. "A little feverish," he said. "But that could be from being buried in this thing," he said tugging down the eiderdown.

"Michael, I'm sure your mother would like your company."

"My mother has gone to the hairdresser. She always goes to him when she comes to New York and then shopping. She likes shopping, too. After that there's dinner with old friends. My mother will not be back for hours and hours."

His hand found the bare flesh of her waist; his fingers spread-eagled, his thumb teasing the warm skin just below her rib. "How are you? Do you really feel ill?"

"Would you really care?" she asked in a low voice.

He moved closer to her. She felt his nakedness with a feeling of fear and pleasure. "Michael, what do you think you are doing?"

"I don't know, but I know what I want to do."

"I'm ill!" she protested weakly.

"Are you really?" He sounded concerned. "Shall I call a doctor?"

She murmured no, she was not that ill. He moved away, lying on his back, an arm at the back of his head. The gesture a familiar one, she closed her eyes against the intensity of feeling that washed over her. Memories flooded her mind, terrifying her. These thoughts weakened any resolve she had to put a distance between them.

She told herself to get out of his way. She should leave the comfort of the bed, yet she was held there in fascination, wondering what he would do, knowing she was on a journey to nowhere with this man. If he did not hate her now, he had hated her once. He had really believed she had left him, and to a man of such machismo that could be considered an unforgivable act. He would have been humiliated in his own eyes, and perhaps even in the eyes of his society. A man who could not hold onto his wife for more than a couple of months? What did that say about him and his virility?

"Michael, let's not do anything we'll regret," she pleaded, at last looking at him. He turned his head, his eyes glowed and they practically scorched her with the intensity of his look. He moved his arm from the back of his head, moving ever so slowly, then turned his body slightly so his hand could very gently stroke her jaw. He cupped her face in his fist, the fingers tracing the flesh beneath her eyes.

"Have you been crying?" he asked his voice low and husky. "Tell me if you are unhappy, please."

"No," she lied, "it's just this bug. I think it's sinus, something like that."

"How romantic, but you feel sad? I guess that's natural, Charley, with everything that has happened to you. You must not be afraid of showing you're sad about your dad. It's natural you would need to mourn him."

She thought, oh, Michael if only you knew what has upset me! Yes, I do mourn my dad but this other thing, what I have learned, that is what is paralysing me. Moments ticked by and all the while her heart dived and plummeted.

She moved ever so slightly, not surprised to feel his flesh against her own. Someone sighed. Michael bent his head and cupped her lips in his.

"You taste of salt," he said.

Then his mouth closed around hers; her head slipping down on the pillow, she offered no resistance. It was only as his hands slid down her, smoothing the soft flesh of her belly, that she sighed her defeat, sliding her arms up around him, arching herself against him, parting her mouth fully, teasing his tongue with her own. He was as he had always been, irresistible to her; something in him awakened all kinds of feelings inside her. She longed to be close to him, remembering how it had been. He had thought she had left him; softly, she melted against him, offering no resistance, as if this would in some way drive away those long and empty bitter years.

His hand playing with her belly drove the heat of desire raging through her, until she was writhing on the bed as his other hand traced the outline of her thighs, causing them to part. She felt a hot melting moisture trickle from her; slowly he slid a hand inside the bikini pants she wore, brushing against her femininity, and then moving on to slide the panties down, manipulating her easily until they slid down her legs.

He knelt before her. In the dull light from a far away lamp, she saw his outline... the broad shoulders, the hair-roughened chest. He slid the panties off her feet before gazing up at her. She lay still, afraid to breath for the long moment he perused her. Ever so gently he placed his palm over her mound, kneeling over her, bending to cup a pouting nipple between his lips and all the while his hand parted and caressed her.

She started to slip into that other world beyond him, beyond sense. She whispered his name, a hurried plea. With a desperate move of her hand, she found him, held him, and caressed him as long ago he had taught her to. He seized hold of her hand and pulled it away from his hard masculinity, folding her arm back and rubbing her wrist with his thumb.

"Baby," he whispered. "I want you so much," he moaned softly at the back of his throat. "Do you want me, baby?"

For an answer, she raised herself up against him, feeling his masculinity against her yielding crevice. Slowly, as if even now trying to stop himself, he slid himself into her. She cried out, rising up to meet him, letting go of the tenuous hold she had on herself, diving into the warm wetness of their complete union.

She tipped wonderfully into the nothingness of reckless pleasure, gasping, floating, her hands tearing down his back, and as she mounted the crest to plunge down, she began again, more slowly this time, riding the wave alongside him, again and again, until with a gasp of triumph he released the last hold on his own ecstasy.

~ * ~

"Baby," he said later, holding her close to him, liking the slippery feel of her drenched skin. Her skin glowed; the round nipples rosy coloured. He moved his hands downwards, into the warm wetness of her centre, feeling the stirring of his loins and marvelling at this woman and what she did to him.

Her wonderful gold coloured eyes widened in surprise as she became aware of the impact she was having on him. He murmured something about it being impossible; her lips parted in a soft smile, her lashes lowering over her eyes. Michael bent and took her lips, caressing them gently, letting himself take his time, enjoying the yearning, until he could hold back no longer against her insistent pleas for fulfilment.

Later he showered as she lay in the tub, relaxing in a maze of heavenly scented bubbles.

"Do you want to eat out?" he asked, leaving the shower and wrapping a towel around his middle. Her eyes were closed. For a moment he thought her sleeping; she raised the lids and looked at him.

She sighed contentedly. "Not really. I could make something," she suggested.

He sat on the edge of the tub. "We can send out," he said. "How about Italian?"

"That would be fine."

He scooped up a handful of bubbles and blew them gently in her direction. She reached up a hand and tried to grasp them, but like him they proved to be elusive.

She slipped into a black velvet pants suit. It was comfortable but she knew the bomber jacket was flattering to her small waist and the trousers emphasised her long slender legs. She put on a little make-up and then large silver earrings that matched the silver buttons of the suit.

Michael was already dressed in pale jeans and a checked shirt. Without formal wear, he looked younger and approachable. His hair glistened with droplets of moisture from his shower; his skin was taut from his shave, his complexion naturally tanned. He was, as she had always found him to be, terribly attractive. He could, even now, make her feel girlish and weak at the knees and with the new knowledge she had about him, dangerous for her peace of mind.

The urge to tell him what his mother had told her bubbled away inside her like a pot on a high burner. Yet what good would it do? As his mother had said, it would ruin his relationship with his family. At least it would for a time. He would be furious with Maria; it would cause a rift. The truth would not do any good for anyone. In time he would come to dislike her for telling the truth; someone

73

who grassed without good motive seldom saw good at the end of it. But her common sense argued back. She had good motives. Those two women had broken them apart, had made both of them so unhappy. Who knew what would have happened if they had not done that? Yet he had never come to seek her out; perhaps in some ways he had not cared enough.

It was too late to change things. Their previous relationship was over; this was not even a relationship. She had entered into a pact so she could keep the hotel running successfully. Love-making had not been part of that pact; it had just happened. He had momentarily wanted her and she had acquiesced.

No, not even that... she had been with him every step of the way. She had wanted him so much, had needed him to hold her, to caress her. There was a void inside her and only he could fill that void.

"You look glum," he said.

"Sorry," she smiled. "I'm not really."

"You really feel under the weather?" he asked with genuine concern, coming across to her.

"No, actually I feel fine." She touched the collar of his shirt lightly; the scent of him teased her nostrils, warm, sweet and masculine. "In fact, you did me good," she blushed, "I mean you made me feel better."

"Glad you added that," he smiled at her. "Come and have a glass of wine. Dinner will be fifteen minutes."

"I love America," she clapped her hands delightedly. "Only in America could I be so spoilt."

He gave her a strange look, long and hard, and then, although it seemed he was about to say something, he turned away and concentrated instead in opening a bottle of red wine.

After they had eaten, Michael went to make coffee; feeling warm and comfortable, Charley sauntered across the luxurious carpet and sat on the sofa. Rain began to beat against the window panes and just as Michael brought the coffee across, a peel of thunder was loud enough to make her start a little.

"Are you okay? Should I close the blinds?"

"No, it just startled me; I like to watch a storm, just so long as I'm indoors."

It was a spectacular storm. Thin streaks of jagged lightning slit open the black sky; then there was loud roar of thunder. Michael came and sat beside her; she felt the light pressure of his arm. There was something reassuring about it.

"I'm scared but I just love it too, sort of like riding on a roller coaster," she confessed.

"You should see it in Florida," he said. "That really is frightening. More coffee?"

"No, that was fine," she put down her cup. Suddenly she felt shy; her heart swelled inside her breast leaving her a little breathless. The glorious intimacy she had shared with him was there in her memory; she was reliving all those tumultuous feelings and, like the storm itself, it thrilled and yet frightened her. Nervously she glanced at him but he was not looking at her. He was staring out at the night sky but she had a feeling he was not even seeing the drama being played before his eyes. He was somewhere else in his mind, far from her.

Tenderness was there now; the urge to just touch him, not to arouse him or to tease him but to be close, to play her fingers through his, to enjoy the warm feel of his flesh against her own. She did nothing and to release her temptation hugged her knees.

His profile was so perfect... his features sculptured; the eight years of maturity had increased rather than decreased his attractiveness. It was terrible to have to admit she had never been able really to get over him. He was her first love, and she had never been able to love anyone else. Always she had said it was because of his betrayal, but it was more than that. He had branded her; her heart belonged to him, it always would. As pathetic as that made her feel, she acknowledged it as the truth.

It would have been so easy to cope if he had not come back into her life. It was her fault he had, and she had made it so he did. It would have been easy to have sold the business as her father had planned but no, she had to throw down a challenge. She had wanted him to come into her arena because she wanted to prove to him she had made a success of her life in spite of everything, and to prove to herself she was really over him after all this time. How ironic, the one thing she desperately needed to prove had proven something else entirely. That she was not and never would be, over him!

It was even worse now that she knew he had not left her so unceremoniously. She had known him so little she had taken the word of those women. Surely, she should have realised a man like him would not have done that. He would have told her straight to her face. The one thing he was not was a coward and yet, the sane part of her insisted, wasn't he using her to rid himself of an ardent admirer? But that was different, she argued. He was desperate because she knew now he had tried everything else.

"What are you thinking about?" he asked, without even turning to look at her.

"Actually, Mercedes. Do you think she has fallen for it? And has she been stalking you?"

"Stalking is a bit of a strong word to use, being persistent would be a kinder way of putting it, but she does seem to turn up wherever I go. Even in London. She seems to think that the more I see her, then that will make me desire her."

"When the opposite is true."

"Precisely."

"I think you could call that stalking."

"She's practically family. I can't call it that," he said, only slightly irritated.

"Anyway, you can tell me tomorrow if you think we've succeeded. Mother and you are having lunch with Mercedes."

The idea of sitting at a table opposite the woman who had helped his sister ruin her life actually made her feel physically sick. There were some things she could do but this thing he demanded was impossible.

"I don't think I'll be doing that." It was a murmured protest but there was steel in it, too.

"Of course you will, look at you..." he said, standing and looking down at her.

"What do you mean, Michael?" she asked placing a hand at her throat. There was something in his expression she had never seen before. She could not really analyse it. It was not anger but it was not happiness either.

"You look so beautiful. You always had that glow after we had made love," he said darkly. "It's there now; I remember that look." And although he smiled, there was no humour or joy in that smile.

"What are you saying?" Charley leapt up from the settee, standing to face him, her hands folded into tight bunches at her hips, afraid she could really strike him if he said something more.

"You know what I'm saying." He was so cool and distant; she felt a lurch at her stomach. Charley had been such a fool, dreaming about him, thinking she might actually have rekindled something. Michael would never really feel anything for her again. He would never forgive her!

"Are you saying you made love to me because you wanted me to look a certain way?" she demanded.

He was quiet for a long time weighing up his answer. He started to speak but paused before saying roughly. "If you want to think that, then do. But not just that, I mean you are still attractive and incredibly..." he hesitated.

"Incredibly what? Naïve seems to fit the bill."

He laughed but there was no humour in it. "Never naïve, I was going to say sexy."

"Bastard," the word spat out from her mouth before she had time to think. It had an immediately effect, making his whole body tense. He glared down at her, his eyes narrowed into slits.

"How dare you! Who in the hell do you think you are?"

"I think I am, in your eyes, no one." She turned away from him, striding purposely across the room. "But it's over."

"It never started, honey, believe me," he said, smooth and cold again.

"You misunderstand," she said, hurting inside and managing only with tremendous will to keep her voice from quavering. "I mean this whole charade. I never thought there was anything in the other thing, Michael, there never was. There was nothing really deep and meaningful, just fun. That was all you ever wanted wasn't it, no commitment and just lots of...?" she shrugged helplessly.

"You know nothing about it or about me," he said. "You never have and you never will."

She went into the bedroom, careful not to slam the door. She took her night things from under the pillow before going into the bathroom for her toothbrush. She expected him to be where she had left him, but when she returned to the living room he was not there. The door to the lobby was open; obviously there was someone at the front door.

She quickly sped across the room and slid quietly into one of the spare bedrooms. There were twin beds, already made up with matching duvets. There was a lock on the inside of the door. She slipped down the catch. Only when she was certain he was locked out did she give into her true feelings. Collapsing on the edge of the bed, she felt weakness sweep over her. Her hands actually trembling, she gripped one hand with the other but the shaking persisted feeling it running through her whole body. She had the urge to cry out but she bit her lips and wondered why she had allowed him to stir up her emotions to such an extent.

He had to really hate her; only someone who hated a person could have spoken like that. He had so little regard for her that he could use her, and then discard her, not simply for his own gratification, which would have been bad enough, but so his own ends could be served. And she had been so easy. Putty in his hands, melting the moment he touched her. He knew what he was doing. He was not that young man anymore; he was someone very different, and she had played such a dangerous game with him.

Later when the trembling subsided and she had some control over her body, she had the satisfying thought that his words had undone his deviousness. For she might have looked radiant an hour or so ago, but his words had blown that radiance to smithereens. Now she was looking pinched and hunched and downright miserable.

After a fitful night, she fell asleep in the early hours of morning; someone's tapping on the outer door wakened her and she pulled herself from the bed, slipping into a robe before going and very cautiously partly opening the door. To her immense relief she saw it was Thelma.

"Coffee for you," she said brightly. After thanking her, Charley took the tray and put it on the floor and locked the door once more. Catching sight of herself in the full length mirror, she saw that there were dark smudges below her eyes, but considering the emotional upheaval she had been through, she did not look too bad. Going closer to the mirror, she viewed herself critically. At the side of her neck there was a faint purple bruise. She almost smiled, but the part smile was bitter. She would go to the luncheon, not for Michael but for herself! She felt a viscous thrill as she thought of what she would say and do. In a way she really needed to somehow punish Mercedes. She would never reveal to Michael what the girl had done, so the only way to really punish her would be to let her think Michael and she were together... forever!

It was turned ten. She took a long leisurely shower, washing her hair, and when she was done, wrapping it in a towel to dry up the excess moisture. After removing the towel, she combed her hair. It was such a good cut it fell immediately into style. If she let it dry naturally, it would look both sleek and shiny.

Amongst the things she had bought was a cheery red trouser suit. It had a fitted jacket and a small velvet collar; importantly she need not wear a blouse with it. She put on a pair of high heeled shoes and merely a modicum of make-up. Her reflection showed her someone who looked quite sophisticated and when she set her expression, someone who did not looked miserable or unhappy. She was not unhappy anyway; she was doing something just for herself and when she had done it, she would make other plans.

Yolanda was already dressed and sitting on the settee waiting for her. Her eyes swept Charley briefly and her greeting was as cool as her assessment of the younger girl. The older woman's prejudice against her did not even wound her; no one could hurt her as much as Michael had. There was a ring of steel around her heart now; she was well protected against anything his mother or Mercedes had to say.

The restaurant was across town and was on the top floor of a tall building overlooking the East River. A maitre d' showed them to their table; he obviously knew Mrs Hernandez. Yolanda ordered a cocktail but Charley requested a glass of sparkling water. She needed to keep her head clear and even one drink at lunch time would go straight to her head. She was sitting opposite Yolanda and when the woman coughed politely and indicated her head in the direction of Charley's neck, Charley met her gaze.

"I know," she smiled, "but what can you do?"

The older woman's lips thinned, but she was prevented from saying anything by the arrival of Mercedes. The small girl was balancing on heels that were too high for her. Her severe black dress without any jewellery, or brightly coloured scarf to lift the dullness, made her look rather severe and widow-like.

In a way, Charley thought, that image is rather appropriate.

Mercedes sat close to Yolanda, trying to hide the maliciousness in her eyes, yet she seemed so furious such duplicity was not possible. When she saw the purple bruise at Charley's throat, her eyes narrowed

"Isn't this jolly?" Charley said taking the proffered menu from the waitress. "And it is so civilised. Really I should punch your lights out, Mercedes, but I can't be bothered." Charley had enjoyed seeing a momentary sparkle of fear come into the other woman's eyes, as if she actually believed Charley might even yet resort to fisticuffs. "Anyway, we ought to drink a toast. What shall we drink to? Ah yes, Michael."

"Really, Charlotte," Mrs Hernandez said. "It is ill becoming of you to behave like this."

"But not ill becoming of Mercedes to conspire and ruin my marriage. Oh, but all to no avail. He doesn't want you, Mercedes, and he wants me. In fact, Michael and I are going to be married the day after tomorrow. And this time no one will come and tell me he doesn't want me anymore, because I know the opposite is true."

"I don't believe he will marry you," Mercedes snapped back, finally finding her tongue. Then she turned to Yolanda and spat out a ream of words in Spanish.

"That's rude, too, Mercedes; you really need to mend your manners."

"Yes, it was very rude, Mercedes. If you have anything to say, you will speak in English. Really, this lunch is turning into something I did not want. I thought we, you and I, Mercedes, had decided you would apologise to Charlotte for what you did."

Being reprimanded by someone she obviously admired caused Mercedes to flush angrily. "Senora, I cannot. I would have done it, but now I cannot apologise to this woman. There is something of the puta about her!"

"Mercedes!" The name exploded from Yolanda Hernandez.

"Don't worry about it, Senora," Charley said, glad to be able to call Michael's mother something that was obviously the norm. "Mercedes can bristle all she likes; she can call me names, too, but it does not alter the fact Michael and I will marry the day after tomorrow."

Yolanda gave Charley a damning look.

Charley felt it unfortunate she had to fool Yolanda Hernandez as well as Mercedes but it could not be helped. She realised too, as she looked at the other girl, she was not enjoying the game. Charley knew she was behaving in a way that she could not admire, and admitting she was putting herself on the girl's level, gave her an unpleasant feeling.

"You will regret it," Mercedes said. "His family will never accept you."

Yolanda Hernandez sucked in a breath. It was very audible and Mercedes turned to look at her.

"You have no right to say that. You cannot and do not and will never speak for my family!" Senora Hernandez said.

Mercedes looked truly wounded; Charley looked down at her plate.

"Senora, you must not be fooled by this woman," Mercedes said. "She is a gold digger, you know this. You said it so often… that gold digging English girl… that is what you called her!"

"Mercedes, please be quiet. What I said I said, but that was in the past. However, Michael is no longer the young boy he was; he is older, very astute and he is a good judge of character. My opposition is based on our different cultures, and I no longer believe Charlotte is a gold digger, if she ever was."

Not to be put down, Mercedes muttered. "You will see; I am afraid you will learn the hard way."

"If Charlotte were a gold digger, then I realise she would have come looking for money. She never has. I admire that about her," Yolanda said very softly, as if she did not even wish Charlotte to hear. Charlotte looked up at Michael's mother; however Yolanda was looking directly at Mercedes.

"There is no point in my being here. I am flying home at five. If you will excuse me, Senora." Mercedes put down her napkin, stood from her chair, and then tottered none too elegantly across the crowded restaurant.

"You did not have to drive the knife in so deep," Yolanda said.

"Yes, I did. I want this over just as much as Michael does."

"What do you mean, over?"

Charley swallowed, unsure what to say. Should she tell his mother the truth? Yolanda already suspected there was no real love affair between her son and his ex-wife. She had said as much. As his mother she had known only too well how Michael felt about the woman he had married and who he imagined had deserted him for no just cause. However, Charley lightly shrugged her shoulders. "Getting Mercedes out of Michael's hair, of course!"

Four

"She's gone now and I am certain that she's out of your life, so I'm going to fly home," she said it all in a rush.

Michael had been sitting in his study off the main lounge area. He had swung his chair around as she entered without knocking, and gave her a quizzical stare. She faltered a little. She had plunged in right away and the words had just tumbled out of her, but now looking at him, long legs stretched out and looking quite at ease, she felt herself weaken in her resolve.

The trouble was, as always he looked devastatingly attractive. He was wearing pale jeans and a checked shirt and should have looked ordinary, yet the casual clothes emphasised his dark attractiveness as well as his masculine build.

It was the first time she had seen him since their bitter encounter the night of the storm. He was out when she arrived home from the lunch with Yolanda and he did not come home for dinner. Yolanda herself had announced she would be leaving on a four o'clock flight to Florida the following day. When Charley heard from Thelma that

Michael was working at home the next morning, Charley decided to have it out with him right away.

"You think?" he said, stretching his body and then swinging his chair a little from side to side.

"I know," she said, the two words come out loud. She was showing him she had regained her strength in argument.

"No deal," he said. "You agreed to do this, Charley; besides, I have other plans for us."

"Oh, you do? That's fine, except I won't be around to take your orders any more. I have fulfilled my part of the bargain and that's that."

"You have fulfilled squat," he said, then he smiled. There was a light in his eye but it was more mischievous than anything else. There was something also too knowing about his smile. "Cat got your tongue?" he asked, because she had not said anything back to him.

"Why are you being like this, Michael?" She could tell her words, spoken calmly, hit home with him for he paled a little, the indolence in his body leaving him.

"Like what?" he asked when he gained his equilibrium.

"I think you know. Anyway, I want to go home, Michael."

"Look, I didn't start it... you did, so now you have to finish it."

"Finish what; I don't know what you mean?"

"You told Mercedes we were to be married, so that's what we're going to do. We're going to get married."

"You have to be mad!"

"Not me. You said it; I never mentioned it. Since you have told my mother and Mercedes that we are to marry, we have to marry. We will be back to where we started otherwise. Tomorrow, we take that drive all over again, up to Connecticut, a quick marriage."

"I absolutely refuse."

"Okay, refuse you may, but if you do, the deal is off."

"To hell with the deal. You keep reneging on it, changing the rules when it suits you."

"Sorry to bore you, but you are the one that made it more difficult. You told Mercedes and you told my mother. I don't intend to disappoint either."

"But what will we do after?" she asked, even though she was determined it was never going to happen.

"After? After, you do what you did before… you walk away, back to England, but at least you will be compensated." He read her expression, saw horror marching across it, and watched as her mouth tried to spit out words. "Yes, I know I am, not actually, Mom and Dad were married, but when it comes to wheeling and dealing, a first rate one, as I've reminded you previously. Calling me names does not worry me, never has actually."

"Michael." She went and sat on a stool nearby, spreading her hands in an imploring gesture.

He watched her, his expression stern, giving nothing away as to what he was thinking.

"This has gotten so out of hand. Mercedes has gone. She has somehow lost the respect of your mother."

"She never had it. A girl that chases after a man? Get real, Charley, you've met my mother!"

Yet his mother had wanted to protect the girl. It was only a moment or two before Charley realised Yolanda was protecting her daughter and not Mercedes. Senora

Hernandez would be quite prepared to throw Mercedes into the lion's den if she had been acting alone, but not her daughter Maria. The family was everything to her. She would not want to cause any rift in that tight knit group.

"But you would be deceiving your mother. You surely would not wish to do that?"

But he shrugged and swung his chair around again to face his computer. "Wear something nice, Charley, like you did last time."

"What is to stop me just going and getting on a plane?" she asked his back.

"Nothing at all. Go do it. Who knows, you might succeed in making something of Blooms Hotel. You have guts enough to try, but I don't have much hope. A lot of guts without cash isn't a lot of use in your situation."

"You really want to punish me, don't you?" She used all her strength to keep her voice steady, though her heart had been accelerating at a frightening pace.

He swung around suddenly. "This has nothing to do with the past," he snapped. "This is to do with the deal you made."

"We didn't make a deal that said I had to marry you."

"That's right. I didn't make any such deal, but like I said, you told them that. It is not my problem. Now if you'll excuse me, I have to finish this work. Then I'm going with Mom to the airport. There's no need for you to come if you don't like."

She stood up and went to leave the room, her mind spinning with ideas and schemes and wanting to get away to write them down.

"And by the way, I've had Thelma strip the beds in the spare room and Mom's room. You stay in my bed until I tell you otherwise."

She knew it would not give her any satisfaction to slam the door as she left the study but she did it anyway.

Once alone in the lounge, she took up pen and paper and sat at the writing desk then tried to work out a scheme for a survival of the hotel without Michael's help. She was still working when Yolanda said she would be leaving and Michael came from the study. Turning the papers over she went to say goodbye to Michael's mother. Charley was mildly surprised when the woman took her by the shoulders and kissed her on each cheek.

"Take care, Charlotte, and take care of Michael too."

The words moved her, more than she had ever thought possible. There was a faint thawing in his mother's attitude that both surprised and touched her. It was the kindness after Michael's mauling of her that left her feeling somehow less vulnerable.

Once they had gone, she returned to the task in hand. She worked on the business plan past the time Thelma said she was leaving. After Thelma left, Charley left her plans and went in search of bedding. She located the linen closet and found sheets and pillows and a comforter. Taking them up, she went back to the bedroom she had used and made up the single bed. "So much for you, Michael," she sniffed as she carried out the task.

"If you think you're staying here, you're sadly mistaken." The voice, low and mellow, not in the least dictatorial, caused her to start. Charley dropped the pillow into which she had been jiggling a brightly coloured pillow slip. Michael was leaning in the doorway, arms folded. She had no idea how long he had been there, watching with that amused expression, as she struggled to make up the bed. She decided to ignore him. Lifting up the case, she eased the pillow inside, and when she was done, her face a mask of defiance, she turned but he had gone.

It came to her suddenly she had left her papers on the writing desk. Speeding out of the room and into the lounge, she saw he was there, where she had dreaded he would be. Michael was standing at the desk going through the papers. More humiliating than his invasion of her privacy was the fact he was actually chuckling as he read.

"Do you mind?" she snapped. Running to his side, she snatched the paperwork from his hands.

He looked at her with amused tolerance as if she was some kind of naughty child. "Let me look, Charley. I might not know much about relationships but I do know the hotel business."

"It's just a rough draft," she muttered.

"You're right about that. Let me try something." He took the papers back from her fingers and spread them out on the desk. Taking up a pen, he whipped through what she had written, crossing out and adding. He was moving figures around quickly as if he had had more than moments to study the plan.

"Now this might work... look." She wanted to say she was not interested, but curiosity got the better of her. She leaned close to him, looking down at the desk, following his finger, listening to what he said. Of course, it made perfect sense.

"Why is it working?" he murmured. He was so close she felt his warm breath against her ear. She stepped back a little and shuffled her feet, making a small distance between them.

"There's an injection of cash. I could make it work that way. I was trying to make it work without the injection of cash. I could have made it work your way," she added, hearing the slightest hint of petulance in her voice and not enjoying it.

"But it just would not work. You would go from one crisis to another, spiralling into debt and not making the improvements the hotel needs. Let's face it, you don't have the experience to do this on your own."

She said nothing; he went on, his voice level and unemotional. "Did your father really want out of the deal? It does not make good business sense, and though he was not the best businessman in the world, he was not an idiot by a long way."

Her first reaction was to lie. What did it matter what Michael believed, and yet she had to be true to her father. She could not lie about him, which would be a wicked thing to do.

"He didn't want to pull out of the deal," she admitted. "He said we would never survive, but he said I could offer up a business plan and he would see. He never got to see my business plan. It was I who pulled out of the deal. The hotel was left to me, so it was my decision."

"Just who were you trying to punish, Charley, me or yourself?" His voice was dark and husky and caused a strange feather of pleasure to erupt all over her body. There were times when Michael sounded as he did when they made love. It was discomforting to realise he did not appreciate what that could do to her feelings.

"I ended up punishing myself, because now I'm stuck with you, unless ..." she turned to look at him. "If I said I would sell out to you, would that be enough to call off our arrangement?"

His eyes swept her. She felt him weighing her carefully as if she was something on display and he was deciding whether to buy or not. Her cheeks flooded red with a mixture of humiliation and anger. Nevertheless she held her stance and though it took all her self control, she did not flinch from his thorough perusal.

"Maybe a couple of days ago. Now it's too late."

"You're impossible," she said with meaning. "And don't think I don't know what this is all about. You want to punish me, punish me for leaving you, that's the honest truth, isn't it?"

"It could be I need to do that, Charley," he said lightly.

"It has to be let go," she said.

He turned and walked away from her. "I have to go out. We'll be leaving at ten in the morning. Don't keep me waiting and do sleep in the spare bedroom. After all, a bridegroom should not see the bride the night before the ceremony. Isn't that right?"

~ * ~

It was sunny yet chilly out. A wind was blowing in from the East River, and he had not put on his overcoat. He turned up the collar of his jacket. Turning off Fifth he headed across town, his back now to the wind. There was a coffee shop he knew and he went inside. They knew him; he just asked for a coffee and sat in a booth. The coffee came quickly. Sometimes the girl chatted to him but she knew when to and when not to. He sipped the hot black liquid, enjoying its bite.

He was a heel. Why was he doing what he was doing to Charlotte? The past was the answer.

But the past was a long time ago, his conscience reminded him. They were just kids and surely it couldn't matter anymore. Sadly it did. It burned him up; she burned him up in more ways than one. It still hurt; the pain was as fresh as it was the day he discovered what she had done.

He only had to think about it, and it was there again. Yet the revenge he had plotted hurt him more than her, he was sure of it. She still turned him on like crazy. One look and it was like a bolt of lightning zinged along his spine. Something about her... her smell, her skin, and the way she moved. Within reason he could have any woman he wanted. It was and always had been easy to find someone but they never made him feel like she did. That was the trouble.

If I hurt her, he had thought, then that will end the spell. It will smash it because revenge could be sweet. Only trouble was, there was a bitter taste in his mouth and he was not supposed to feel this way. Of course it was his fault. Hell, he made her sleep in his bed. It was more agony for him than it ever would be for her. Well, that was over; there would be no more of that. At least then he could keep a clear head.

He picked up his cell phone and stared at it. He thought he would call her and call the whole marriage thing off. It was ridiculous to make her go through with it but then he thought, I've gone this far and Mercedes is almost gone.

He would not have to call the police about her. Mercedes' crazy letters and phone calls were getting frightening. She could not seem to understand how he had gone from being her friend to positively loathing her. But none of that was Charley's fault. No, he reasoned to himself, but she could help me with a problem. It was not much to ask after what Charley had done to him. Hell, he was going mad! He keyed in some numbers. They answered at the Inn. "Michael Hernandez here. Do you have a twin room?" he asked, "I'd like to change it from the double I booked."

~ * ~

Charley had to keep reminding herself that, although he wished to humiliate her, Michael was not setting out to hurt her. The fact he took her as his wife a second time, at the same place as previously, had nothing to do with it. Michael believed she had left him because she did not love him anymore. How could he be anticipating causing her any anguish? If he was punishing anyone, then it was himself. That she could not understand. This masochism was not like him at all, yet there seemed no other explanation for his choice of venue. Unless, and she doubted it, he had not realised it was the same place!

The trees around the white New England house were a riot of colour; it was the end of the fall and the trees were ready to lose their leaves, but just now they were in the dying days of their glory. Reds of all hues, dark and pale gold. The fantastic sight of New England in the fall never failed to make her feel good. Even today of all days, she felt something warm and glowing at the core of her. It was the joy she received from glorifying in nature, and, unlike with other brides, it had nothing to do with the man she was marrying.

It was not the same Justice that performed the ceremony. This one was much younger... probably, she mused, the first one's son. Now that really would be something to tell her grandchildren except she would not be having any grandchildren, not ever and not with the man she was marrying. Her future, she knew, would be bleak. Her career would be the only consolation for her loneliness.

They offered the service of taking a photograph and, surprising her, Michael went for it, ordering ten photographs, one he said for important members of his family and their friends. She knew by friends he meant to include Mercedes and her father.

He had driven himself; they had taken the Parkway which always was a favourite route of hers, but instead of driving right back to New York, he turned off near Greenwich and, after traversing some country lanes, pulled up outside an Inn. It was an old New England mansion; stylish and comfortable but to her question as to whether it was in his chain, he said no. He wanted to be incognito.

Inside there was a comfortable lounge with an open fire, the logs blazing in the huge grate. She loved the colonial style of the place; it gave out a wonderful welcoming atmosphere. Apparently, he had made a booking and had packed a small case that a porter brought from the boot of the car.

"You should have warned me. I haven't anything."

"You don't need anything. I brought everything you need."

"Like what, a jar of arsenic?" she quipped. He smiled that half smile he had but made no further comment.

She knew before she reached their room it would be a double. She sensed he would do that just to put her on her mettle. It was a huge room with a four poster bed and a huge comfy looking sofa. She eyed that and thought it would be very comfortable for sleeping on. The central heating was ticking over pleasantly but there was also an open fire in the room, already lit and with a basket of logs to keep it going.

After the porter had left, pocketing a large tip, Michael snapped open the case. He took out a brightly coloured toilet bag and went through a door she assumed led to the bathroom. Her insatiable curiosity led her to take a look in the bag. There were some lingerie items for her and she spluttered some unpleasant words under her breath at Michael's temerity! How dare he go riffling through her underwear.

She pulled the garments out and noticed they were the flimsiest, fanciest pieces she owned. Under the lingerie was a pair of dark brown trousers and a tan cashmere sweater. She pulled those out and a pair of brown boots. There was nothing else of hers so she presumed her toothbrush and other items were in the toilet bag he had taken into the bathroom.

For her wedding, she had chosen to wear the dark green woollen suit she had bought with the personal shopper's help. It was smart and business-like; she thought it complemented their marriage... it was a business arrangement and nothing more. Yet catching a glimpse of herself in the mirror, she had to admit the suit not only suited her figure but her complexion. It was a very becoming outfit, and she had not realised that until just now. Damn the man! He would think she was obeying his dictates she wear something nice!

A discreet knock at the door brought Michael from the bathroom. He let in the same porter who was carrying an ice bucket and inside the ice bucket she saw there was a bottle of champagne. A young girl followed him carrying some titbits on another tray, together with glasses and napkins. The porter announced that dinner would be served at seven and a table had been reserved by the fire as requested. Then, when Michael said he would open the champagne, the waiter and the girl left.

Instead of saying anything, Charley went into the bathroom. Their stuff had been put out… there was bubble bath and ordinary soap, Michael's shaving things and some perfume and deodorant for each as well as her toothbrush and toothpaste. He had thought of everything. Uncharitably she thought to herself, just typical! She lifted up a flannel and ran it under the cold tap, and after squeezing all the water from it, held it against first one cheek and then another.

It was hard not to think about their first honeymoon. Then it had been back at the small apartment they had rented. There was no champagne, just a bottle of cool white wine and some cheese straw things, and then later they had steak and salad. It was such simple but wonderful fare. She had been so deliriously happy.

Their love making was a revelation. She had been a virgin and he had taken so long over entering her there had been hardly any pain. There had been a little blood. She had felt oddly humiliated. Michael though had held her to him and told her it was merely confirmation, as if he had needed any, that she had waited for the right man to come along.

"Charley, come and have some champagne."

"What have I to celebrate?" she muttered, but quietly so only she could hear. With a little grimace, she went out to join him and took the proffered glass.

"Here's to Blooms," he said, "it really is going to be something. The more I think about it, the more excited I get."

It was a sweet toast, even feeling as she did about everything, she had to concede that. It was important that Blooms was a success; she wanted it for her father and for his loyal staff, who had stayed with him through all the good and the bad times. It made even this charade seem worthwhile when she thought about it like that.

"You look gorgeous," he said, "but you know that. Green is your colour. I don't think I ever met anyone who suited green as much as you, even including red heads. I think it has to do with your being the nut brown maid, trees and all," he smiled.

"Trying to sweet talk me into bed, Michael?" she said, unable to stop herself from being cynical.

"No need to do that, honey, all I have to do is..." he was closer to her now, she went to step back but he took the glass of champagne from her hand, set it on the table and seized hold of her, taking her lips in his own.

His kiss wrung every vestige of willpower out of her. She stayed still, did not let her lips part, not even as his tongue very lightly brushed along her upper lip, causing wondrous sensations to erupt right through her. The sensual feelings zipped down to her toes that curled defensively against the soft leather of her shoes. She longed to drown in his mouth, to bend her body to his, but she would not. Just when the pain of not yielding became almost too great, he released her very gently.

Michael stepped back, moving away from her, then lifted her glass of champagne and placed it back in her hand.

"Fine," he said, "play hard to get if you want. But at least I am honest enough to admit when I look at you something goes pow!"

"I wasn't playing anything, Michael. And I do know what goes pow and it has nothing to do with your mind. Anyway, I just did not want to be kissed by you, or come to that, by anyone."

"Going to be a nun?" he asked, but he did not wait for her answer. "Have some more champagne." He poured more into her glass then went and refilled his own. "I think I'll take a bath before dinner," he said, then crossed towards the bathroom. "Coming?"

"You've got to be..." but he cut in with a rather mischievous grin.

"Joking?"

"Absolutely."

"Pity, it's a real big tub."

"Suitable for a mammoth ego," she said. This time he did not respond. She listened to the taps running, then slipped out of her shoes and went and sat in the comfy chair by the fire. It was coming up to six; there was a television and she put on the news, now and again picking at the nibbles that had come with the champagne.

Michael was not long coming back. He came in wearing a white towelling robe with his hair damp and tousled, looking devastatingly attractive. He had for her that thing, that mysterious whatever it was, that caused explosions of delight to cascade through her when she looked at him. The tiny sips of champagne she had taken were weakening her resolve and she almost found herself longing to run up to him, to take him in her arms and hold him, to run her hands over his skin. She knew how it would feel after his bath, soft and warm and he would smell and taste delicious.

"Are you having a bath or anything?" he asked, "Only dinner is at seven, you know how early they like to eat in the country."

"I'll take a shower," she said, and sped quickly across the carpet, terrified of the feelings that had started to erupt.

In spite of it being late autumn, she took a cold shower, attempting to douse the warm and wonderful feelings that had erupted when she had looked at him. This is just a game to him, she counselled herself. He will never care about you. You are the woman whom he thinks walked out on him. He had to have loved you then and love like that never forgets the hurt. He will keep on trying to punish you just in case this will assuage that hurt. There will be no let up because those feelings of hate and hurt will never leave him where you are concerned.

Unjustified as they are, they are real to him, so keep your wits about you, girl. She rubbed herself hard with the towel, leaving red marks across her body but she needed to do that, to drive out the tender feelings just below the surface.

The table set for them was in an alcove to the right of the fire facing the window. The napery was dark cream and the cutlery silver. There were crystal glasses. In a silver vase was a single long stemmed, tightly budded crimson rose. The light from a cream candle gave a warm glow as well as the flicker of red flames from the fire.

There were other diners but they were at the other side of the room. Michael had his back to the room, while she sat facing him and the room. The waiter was discreet, the menu extensive. As she folded the menu's cover, the glint of gold caught her eye; it was her wedding ring, a thick gold band, plain but heavy. Michael wore one, too; he certainly was playing the game straight. When they had been married previously he had not worn a wedding band.

When she gave her order, Michael ordered a red wine. They did not speak nor did he look at her. Their starters soon came, hers a salad. She felt a faint pang of hunger and realised she had not eaten anything apart from a slice of toast and the nibbles in their room, yet it was hard to enjoy the food when she felt so uncomfortable. The thought of after dinner haunted her. If she looked at him, she knew she would feel that delicious weakening at her limbs, that teasing tantalising movement over her stomach, the melting of her resolve to have nothing to do with him. It was very difficult to muster strength to resist him and if he touched her, she feared she would be lost once more.

Yet perhaps he would not; the coldness had come down over him again. He made no attempt to converse with her, or put on the charm she knew him capable of. He was very different from how he had been in the room and she did not believe it was because there were diners in the room. Michael would not be swayed by anyone from showing he cared, if that was what he wanted to do. He had never minded displaying his feelings for her, no matter who was around.

She occupied herself by surmising about the other diners, who they were, where they came from, what they did. They looked for the most part middle-aged and settled, probably, she thought, people who lived locally come out for an evening meal. There were two couples who were more than likely tourists.

In spite of her feelings, she managed to finish her salad but when the main course came, she knew she would never be able to do justice to it. The food was really good and she, feeling she should say something positive, said so to Michael. At last he looked up at her. His dark eyes were full of light, sparkling with the reflection of the candle and the firelight.

"Yes, this Inn is renowned for its cuisine. The chef, Bob isn't it? At Blooms... he's a good cook. I wonder he stayed with you. He has the potential to go far. I am not being sarcastic, but he could work anywhere, London for example."

"I know," she admitted. "But he likes living in the town; he has a wife and they have two children who are settled in school. He has an elderly father too I think it's these family ties that keep him, and a sense of loyalty. He came to Blooms straight from school and did his training with Dad's previous chef, as well as going on day release to college. Dad always believed wherever possible in promoting from within."

"A good policy. He really is an asset to the hotel. You need to promote him once you start up again. There are all kinds of things you can do For example you can have him cook for local special occasions. You could offer courses for cooking and have food focus events."

She felt a momentary and enlivening enthusiasm. It was what she had been planning, one of the things she had talked about with her father. It was not good enough just to have Bob cook for residents and diners; you had to reach out further than that. She said as much to Michael, divulging the things she had been thinking about. He listened, nodded now and again and in the end gave his approval. Not that she needed it, but he was such an expert it was good to know she was not as stupid as she had imagined he thought her to be.

Since they had been talking, she had eaten more than she had thought she could. If she was not worrying about him and the effect he was having on her physically, then she found she could behave like a rational human being. However, she refused pudding and opted for a coffee. Michael did the same.

She was starting to feel quite complacent about everything, finding some equilibrium but he had to ruin it by saying, in that dark chocolate voice he saved for when he wanted to stir her up into a whirl of confusion.

"And what would you like to do this evening?"

Hoping the dim lighting saved her blushes, she replied rather pertly. "I think I'd like to go for a walk."

"Why not," he said. "We can cross the river by the covered bridge and then stroll down into town. They have a main street here rather than a Mall. It's quite attractive."

"Lovely," she said brightly.

"I'll get your coat," he said.

"Oh, I did not bring a coat," she murmured, a hint of disappointment in her voice. She knew enough about New England in the fall to know there would be a savage nip in the evening air and her suit was hardly warm enough to go out in.

"I brought your coat," he said. "It's in the boot of the car, together with mine. Wait here."

It would have been lovely to have snapped sarcastically, "How thoughtful of you," but then she realised it was really thoughtful; there was no need for sarcasm. Had he not thought of it, she would have had to call off the walk.

He came back in his black cashmere overcoat, carrying her white cashmere jacket over his arm. She stood and he held the coat for her to slip her arms in, and then gently eased the coat onto her shoulders.

The sky was littered with stars; the night was so clear and fresh. The bridge was draped with fairy lights; some leaves were drifting down from the trees in a chilly but soft breeze. Soon all the trees would drop and the paths and roads would be piled high with russet and golden leaves; there would be the smell of log fires. She loved autumn in the east… there was something so special about it.

Main Street was pretty. At the far end of the street was a white painted church. The shops had lights in the windows; there were no steel shutters. It was a country idyll.

"I could really live somewhere like this," she sighed, barely aware she had spoken out loud. However, perhaps she thought she had really whispered the words, for Michael said nothing.

When they reached the end of the street, they turned and began to stroll back. There was no one about, not even a passing car. Each step drawing them towards the Inn brought her closer to their room. Panic started to well up inside her. She thought of the couch and vowed she would sleep there. Yet, if he touched her, caressed her, she would never be able to resist as she had done earlier in the evening. Somehow his sensuality was wrapping itself around her, tugging at her, invading her. He was not even touching her, or walking particularly close but it was there, an invisible thread drawing her into his web.

When they reached the lobby at the Inn, Michael turned to her. "I have some calls to make, you go ahead."

Once inside the room, she checked the closets for extra blankets. There were some and also pillows. She looked at the couch, then at the bed. A warming fizzle of delight burned along her spine, a tugging deep inside her told her all she needed to know. She wanted him, wanted him so badly her legs could barely support her.

A thin, transparent cream negligée lay across her pillow. It was new. She lifted the filmy garment, marvelling at its sensual feel. There was a matching peignoir, although here, sections of cobwebs of lace allowed more covering. He had to have bought it for her. The realisation merely increased the warm liquid feelings deep within her. But he hated her, she knew that, and yet he was drawn to her, too. There was no hate in his love-making; he had been so tender, so loving, caressing her gently, arousing her. There had been no desire to hurt her in his touch, no viciousness, no cruelty. She hesitated but really she knew her mind was made up.

Hastily she removed her clothing; slipping the thin slivers of silk over her body, thrilling to the sensuous feel of the material. A glimpse of herself in the mirror showed her just how well he knew her body for the garment fitted perfectly where it was supposed to fit and flowed where it was supposed to flow. A momentary wave of shyness caused her to slide into the peignoir, then with fingers that were unsteady, to fasten the tiny pearl buttons at her breasts. Here the peignoir covered her, the hand-sewn lace hugging but not revealing her breasts.

Hurriedly she hung up her suit and put it in the wardrobe, paused at the dressing table to dab a little scent at her wrists and crossed to the bed. It was a high bed with a canopy. She climbed in, tucking the comforter around her and lay back against the pillows. She kept one lamp on low; the flickering shadows came from the logs burning in the grate. She lay watching the waves of shadow dance across the walls.

The silence made her feel drowsy. It seemed a long time had passed and still he had not come. How many calls was he making and to whom? A glance at the clock told her it was now turned eleven. Her eyelids flickered; she closed her eyes, just for a moment relaxing in the deep comfort of the bed.

It was very dark. Her eyes opened, the fire had died, and the low pink light had been extinguished. Slowly she turned in the bed, reaching out an arm. It was a large bed but even so, where her arm touched was cold. She pulled herself up; it was too dark to see anything. Stretching out a hand, she found the switch on a small bedside lamp. Once the switch was pressed, a dull light partly illuminated the room. She pushed back the comforter and lowered her feet to the floor. In spite of the central heating, the carpet felt rather cool. The clock showed the time as five past four.

The light in the bathroom was not on, but the door was open. She was certain she had closed it. Stealthily crossing the floor, she came around the couch. Michael was there, a comforter wrapped around him and a pillow at his head. He was fast asleep. A little gasp escaped from between her lips. Quickly she turned and sped back to bed. Climbing in she pulled the comforter around her. Her heart was beating wildly. She placed a hand at her chest as if to still the frightening thud.

Disappointment washed over her. It was easy to recognize it, and it was something she had had experience of before. Yet why should she be disappointed? It was what she had wanted. When he had kissed her earlier she had managed to keep cool and cold, forcing herself not to melt against him. He had obviously taken the hint. Yet that was not what she had wanted when she had come to the room last night. "What do you want, girl?" she asked herself. But she knew the answer. She wanted to be close to him; wanted him inside her. The shock of the admission caused her to turn restlessly in the bed. Her whole body seemed to burst into flames from the longing deep inside her. No matter how she tossed or turned in the bed, there was no release. The more she tried to suppress the yearning, the fiercer that yearning became.

Unable to bear it, she left the bed once more, tip-toeing across the carpet. His arm was outside the comforter, lying across his chest. Timidly she touched it; it felt a little cold. She cupped it at the wrist thinking she would tuck it under the covers, but he turned restlessly, not quite awake. The movement caused the comforter to slide from his shoulder, revealing burnished bare flesh, his strong shoulders and broad chest, the smattering of dark curling hair. Her tongue nervously circled her upper lip as she stood for a moment listening to her own heart beat.

Falling to her knees, she slid her hand across his chest, slowly, tenderly smoothing the palm against the hair and skin. Her middle finger found the taut nipple and made soft circles over the surface. He moaned deep in this throat, straightening his bent legs and moving restlessly.

"Michael," she murmured ever so softly.

"Mm?" He sounded drowsy and still half asleep.

His body felt good against her searching fingers, the skin so taut and smooth and warm. Her hand slid down his ribcage, finding the last rib and then smoothing its way back up again. When she turned to look at him, she almost fled with the shock of finding him awake, his eyes boring into her. Before she could say anything, his arms moved, pulling her close to him, so roughly she almost toppled over. He was so strong, even in that supine position, well able to manipulate her off her knees and to bring her on top of him. His hands were in her hair, drawing down her head until her lips met his and they blended. Her lips parted at his first touch, her tongue answering his.

Somehow he rolled with her onto the floor, following the comforter that was tangled around them, softening the fall. Immediately his hands sought her, pulling apart the tiny pearl buttons on the peignoir, in spite of its obvious expense, ripping it from her. The thin silk of the negligée caressed her body as his hands manipulated it, smoothing it over breasts, raising her arms and sliding her out of it, while one of his legs slid between her own. The explosion inside her came at once. The moment she felt his flesh against her moist centre, she groaned, moving against him, unable to hold back. His mouth slid down her, cupping and nibbling the soft flesh of her belly, and then sliding against the warm wetness, driving her to the dizzy heights of ecstasy.

He came to claim her lips once more, his hands smoothing over her, caressing the full swell of her breasts, teasing the nipples with his thumbs. Her body thrashed against his once more, her kisses begging him, teasing him, her hands kneading the flesh of his back.

"I want you so much," he ground out to her, his voice broken and his breath coming in short gasps. It sounded as if he did not quite believe just how much he wanted her. She felt a moment's triumph, for whatever else they thought, there was something still there beneath it all, a spark of desire. He wanted her, and oh, how she wanted him. As if in answer, she parted her legs, rising up against him and something snapped, some kind of ridiculous self control that he had been maintaining shattered. He mumbled words that were not English, as if he had lost complete control of who he was. He took her, sliding deep within her, taking her with him into an explosion of delight. She could not stop words from tumbling from her, nor hold back. She said his name... Michael, Michael and heard him cry, "angel, my angel," in reply.

Five

She was on her own most of the time, hardly seeing Michael. If you were going to be on your own, she reasoned, then New York was the place to be. There were lots of things for her to do. She went to galleries and walked the city streets, marvelling at the sites like a tourist. She visited places she had never been when she had lived in Westchester, like going on the ferry to the Statue of Liberty just for the fun of it. Then there was Chinatown. It was easy to get about; she rode the subway as if born to it.

The worst days were those when the rain thrashed down. It was a distance to the subway and she did not like to take a taxi. Those days she read and spent time at the gym in the building.

All these things she did to make time pass. She did wonder when Michael was going to let her go home. After all, it was not as if he were taking her out with him. In fact, she knew he was avoiding her. He seldom came home until she had turned in and, although he shared her bed, he was gone before she was awake. He did not attempt to repeat what had happened at the Inn. Neither did she.

At first she had waited to see what would happen. After that night of passionate love-making, she thought he would reach for her; he never had. She had made the initial overtures and now he was letting her know it had not been his idea to consummate their marriage.

It was clear he regretted making love to her when they had first been in New York. In the early hours of the morning in Connecticut on their so called honeymoon, he had been caught at a vulnerable moment. He was certainly making sure he was no longer that vulnerable. He was always pleasant and polite and he had been the next morning, but that was all. He never referred to anything remotely physical.

The thought that was always crossing her mind was if she told him the truth, would it make a difference? And did she care, she questioned herself, enough to want to make that difference? Of course, she was terrified of admitting it would make the world of difference to her. She wanted him to think well of her, wanted him to know, so desperately it hurt, that she had not left him of her own volition. That her feelings now were as strong as they had been when she had believed he had broken her heart.

"Oh, Michael," she murmured into the empty night. "What have you done to me?"

The nights had drawn in; the air was much colder. They would soon be into December and then what? Her two months were nearly up and yet only that morning a delivery man had arrived at the door, accompanied by the doorman, with a rack of winter coats. She had to choose two, he said, and he would leave them with her. He gave her a card to call him when she had made her choice.

The racks of coats were obviously straight from a design house, classic designs in a range of vivid colour. One, different from the rest, was a speckled pale tweed affair with a deep piled fur collar. They were all in her size, each one with a satin lining and with a prestigious label. It was not that she did not need a good winter coat, for the cashmere jacket she had would not be suitable for a ten below temperature. Yet she could not see the point in choosing a coat, let alone two, as she would be going home soon.

If she bought a thick sweater, that would see her through until she left. However, she tried on the coats. The speckled tweed and a bottle green classic style appealed most. She made up her mind to choose just one; after all, she needed to go out of the apartment.

She tried the speckled tweed again. It had a nipped in waist and a tie belt and certainly suited her figure and colouring. Yet the bottle green classic was just that, a classic coat with a style and cut that would last her a lifetime. She was so engrossed she did not hear the door open and close, but there was a prickling sensation at her neck and when she turned from the mirror, it was to see Michael leaning against the door frame in a nonchalant manner.

"Mm," he said, "suits you."

"It is nice," she admitted shyly, turning up the collar to her face to feel it against her skin, unaware of the sensuality of the movement.

"What other do you like?" He asked, still lounging.

"I was going to take just the one," she murmured, "it's not as if I'm going to need two winter coats in England." A nervous laugh followed the statement, as if it were a joke. She really detested that laugh and wish she could draw it back inside her.

"Take two. While you're here I would not like you going around in the same coat. People would think me a skinflint!"

"That you are not," she declared. She did not feel like arguing with him. She had a mad desire just to please him. She shrugged out of the coat and pulled the bottle green classic coat from its hanger. "I like this, too," she said, shrugging into it.

"Good choice," he said. "I'll call them." He turned to leave, got half way out of the door, then paused and called over his shoulder. "You might like to pack a toilet bag and some underwear. We leave in an hour."

"What?"

She trailed out and by the time she reached the living room, he was already on the phone telling them they should come and collect the rest of the coats. He would be leaving in an hour and the doorman would have the key to let them in.

Seeing her there, he asked, after putting down the phone. "Shouldn't you be getting ready?"

"Where am I supposed to be going?" she asked, exasperated. "And do I need more than a night's things? Aren't I entitled to some information?"

"Sure," he shrugged. "We're going home."

"To England? Then why do I need a coat for New York weather?"

"Home… my home in Florida."

"Florida?"

"Sure, it's Thanksgiving; you know the family always gets together for Thanksgiving."

"Thanksgiving?" She searched her mind for the date. Of course. Thanksgiving was the fourth Thursday in November. Today was Tuesday. Then other things popped up in her mind… family, the family, all together.

"Do you mean your whole family is going to be there?"

"Of course," he said. "At my Mom's house, but we stay at my house, okay?"

"I don't think I can do this, Michael." She was thinking of Maria. The girl's face came to her, that beautiful dark girl, the eyes so large and dark, the perfect honey toasted skin and the immaculate clothes. The way her thin lips had almost sneered out the news Michael no longer wanted her.

"Sure you can. You have to. Believe me, I would not insist if I thought it not necessary. Besides, you didn't say you wouldn't come."

"I don't understand, Michael. This is the first I've heard about it."

"What? I left you a note." He turned and left the room, going to the kitchen. She followed. "Here it is on the 'fridge."

She stood next to him, reading the note. "Charley, I think we have to go to Mom's for Thanksgiving. Call me if you have a problem." And then there was a phone number.

"I didn't see it."

"I'm sorry, Charley. I should have called you. It's just that..." he hesitated. "Life has been a bit fraught. Okay, we don't have to go if you don't want. It's my fault for not talking it through with you."

She looked at him and thought of how important Thanksgiving was. She knew it was a special time for families to be together.

"No, we can go; it's all right. I just never checked the 'fridge and Thelma never mentioned anything when she brought my coffee. How long has it been there?"

"Yesterday. I should have called you, Charley, but I have been so damn busy and I felt sure you'd see it. I know you don't take milk but surely you drink soda?"

"No, it seems to be gassier than I am used to and upset my stomach. Never mind, Michael. It was just one of those things. I'm afraid I ate out yesterday and went to bed early."

"No harm done. I couldn't mention it earlier. I was tied up on things and I was not even sure we could get away."

"Don't worry about it, Michael, really it is okay. What kinds of clothes will I need? Will it be warm?"

"We can get stuff there... it will be warm. Just bring little stuff like lingerie and you might like to travel in something light but wear one of your new coats to the airport. It's pretty cold outside." Michael went to the telephone again and started to key in numbers.

Charley had thought they would travel scheduled airlines. However, when they reached the airport it was to a landing field that was home to private jets. Again her confidence started to ebb away.

The steward that came to greet them wore a white jacket and just to the right of him was the pilot. Michael formally introduced her to both as his wife, Mrs Hernandez. They welcomed her on board and said they hoped she would find the flight a pleasure. Charley knew she would not; she was a nervous flyer anyway, and the thought of being in this small plane terrified her. However, once inside, its opulent comfort set her mind at ease marginally. She had imagined there would be no fancy fittings, that it would be like the planes of World War II and she would have to sit behind the pilot. She saw how silly that idea had been. Here there were cream leather seats, deep and comfortable, television, books, a cocktail bar, and in another small alcove a place to eat. There was, Michael said, even a separate bedroom, but since it was not a long flight, there was no need to use that. "Unless…" he added.

Her heart thudded as she imagined the reality of his words. The reckless beat immediately stilled, however, when he said in the off-handed tone he could sometimes use to her.

"You look real tired. Would you like a nap?"

"I'm fine," she murmured.

She went to take off her coat, but the steward was immediately there, helping her off with it. She was glad she had chosen to wear the navy and white silk jersey pants suit and not a leisure suit she had considered.

"Would you care for a drink, Ma'am?" the steward asked, giving her a warm smile that made her think he should be modelling in a catalogue rather than working as an air steward.

She thought of the turbulence in her stomach and asked for a glass of wine, red if he had it.

"I'll have wine too, Col; open up a bottle of my special, and I'll have salad to eat, chicken I think, after we've taken off. Charley, what would you like? There's a menu." He gave her a brief warm smile, then turning back to the steward said. "I think Mrs Hernandez would like a drink before we take off. She looks a tad apprehensive, don't you think?"

Col said nothing but inclined his head and disappeared into what she assumed was the galley.

"Okay, I am a little scared, but there was no need for you to broadcast the fact."

"He could see it himself and don't tell me you don't need a drink or something,"

"I certainly do."

"Don't worry; you're safer than when I'm driving."

"Is that supposed to reassure me?" she murmured back. The anticipated retaliation did not come and when she looked at him, she saw he had picked up a newspaper and was scanning it nonchalantly. When Col came back, she ordered just salad, no chicken. She did not think she would be able to do more than just pick at the food anyway.

The crazy thought came into her head that if they died on their journey, if something happened to the plane, which in her mind seemed quite likely, then he would die never knowing how much she had loved him. How she had not deserted him at all but had been driven away by two very spiteful women.

"Michael," she said, he turned his head to glance at her. She could not do it; the words would not come.

He raised an eyebrow at her, and then when he saw she would say nothing else, he turned his attention back to the paper.

She took a grateful sip of wine. She had almost done it, almost let the words out. It was serious and the laughter inside had more to do with hysteria than humour, but she had the sudden thought that if she had told him and they had survived the journey, what an eventful Thanksgiving Day it would have turned out to be.

When the plane touched down at Tampa, it was early evening. As they left the confines of the airport, the warm gushing air wrapped itself around her and gratefully she shrugged out of her coat. She liked the feel of the balmy air, the warm enveloping feeling it gave to her.

A car was waiting for them, a large American model with a uniformed chauffeur. Again Michael paused to introduce her as his wife and the man tipped his hat and smiled at her warmly. When he spoke to acknowledge her, his accent was a slow, deep southern drawl she found appealing. Michael, although he had always professed not to be a Yankee, had lost his accent. Now and again or when he was angry, it came to the surface but really his accent was quite indistinguishable from any well educated American, at least to her ears.

Once the confines of downtown Tampa were passed through, they sped north along a highway. When they left the main highway, they took on a narrow road with trees on either side. The moonlight was very bright and she could see the pale blond moss hanging from the trees in sparkling spirals. The landscape was flat but in daylight she imagined it would be quite green. There seemed to be lots of fields and open spaces, not something she had associated with Florida.

Eventually the huge car swung toward some high gates. The driver had to have pressed something in the car, for the gates swung open at their approach. They travelled a long drive that had a curve in it; when they took the curve, she saw through the front windscreen a huge white mansion. It was the most beautiful house she thought she had ever seen. She said. "Gone with the Wind."

And Michael laughed. "Sort of," he said. "But this is new, well, six years old is all."

Immediately the car pulled up, the front door opened and three people stepped onto the terrace. The white porticoes supported a covered roof that gave shade to the terrace. There were pots of brightly coloured plants, a sofa and chairs and a wrought iron table and chair set. The floor was of brightly coloured tiles and the whole area was illuminated by discreet lanterns.

The people that had come out and to whom Michael introduced her were of Hispanic origin... an older couple and a younger woman who was obviously some relation of theirs. They greeted her in hesitant English. The older of the women said she should come in and she would show her the house.

"You can leave that, Consuela, until tomorrow. Mrs Hernandez is tired. I'll take her up to our room and you can bring... what would you like, honey?"

"Tea would be good," she said, "if that's okay."

"Sure it's okay," Michael said pleasantly, and she knew it was more for the servant's benefit than for hers. "Now would I be married to an English woman without making sure that tea was on offer? I wouldn't dare do otherwise, would I?"

She felt like saying "Don't overplay it." The theatrics seemed just a little over the top, but she just smiled and said it would be lovely.

"Consuela will bring it to our room. I'll have some of your special chocolate, Consuela. You know only you can make chocolate as I like it." The woman giggled pleasantly and bustled off to see to what she had to do. "Just bring up the bags, Philippe. Come on, honey, you must be really bushed."

The truth was she felt exhausted. The flight, in spite of her misgiving, had been really pleasant and the food delicious. It was not that late, but she felt as if it were about two in the morning. Philippe, who was much older than she, charged up the stairs in front of her, and Michael, not hindered by carrying a laptop and a small briefcase, had a steady pace, yet she felt she was dragging herself sluggishly up the stairway. It was a wide gracious stairway with highly polished handrails; it curved and the first floor showed a long corridor that went left and right. The staircase went onto a second floor and there was, Michael told her, a third. Thankfully, they went only to the first floor following Philippe to the right. At the end of the hallway were double doors. Philippe opened them both and swept inside. He was on his way out just before she reached the room.

It was an enormous room, the floors wooden with scatter rugs, a sofa and two armchairs, a table and a writing desk and the bed, king-sized with a canopy and white satin hangings you could pull around the bed to make it even more private. The windows had white louvered doors; these were open. Going to look through the screened glass, she saw there was a long wide balcony. There were chairs outside and lights sparkled below on a huge turquoise pool.

Michael came to her side and quietly closed the louvered doors. "Each window has louvers. They keep the room cool during the day and we have a cooler if you find it too hot, but this time of year it's pretty good without the cooler. If you feel you need it, just press this switch and it'll come on." He showed her the switch. "Come on, this is the bathroom." He took her hand. She felt so weary she did not even appreciate fully the little thrill that his touch awoke.

Across the room, doors let into a huge bathroom. There was a large sunken tub in white porcelain with a black marble surround; two showers, a black marble topped vanity unit with two sinks and lots of cupboard space. The tiled floor was enlivened by black and white rugs. Back in the bedroom were two walk in closets. Inside hers were a couple of sun-dresses and several sun-tops and shorts as well as a few swimsuits and bikinis.

At her look in his direction, he said. "I ordered a couple of things. If you don't like them we can change them tomorrow."

"Thank you," she said quietly. "Michael, I think I'll take a bath if you don't mind, then have some tea and turn in."

"Sure. You do that. You look a little drawn. Are you okay?" he asked with kindness.

"I'm fine, just tired," she said with a shrug.

"I have calls to make and e-mails to attend to. Work never stops; I'll see you in the morning."

"You don't stay here?"

"Here? Sure I do. My God can you imagine what old Consuela would say if I didn't share your bed? I meant I'll be late; you'll probably be asleep."

You mean you hope I'm asleep, but she did not give life to the words. There was no point. It would mean nothing to him and anyway, he was right this time. She would be asleep. She felt as if she could sleep for days.

~ * ~

She had swum fifteen lengths when she felt tiredness washing over her. Charley moved sluggishly to the steps and slowly heaved herself out of the water. She ambled to the patio area, where she had left her wrap skirt. The only swimsuits in the closet were all the briefest of bikinis. Charley quickly tied the skirt around her, then after towelling her shoulders dry, she lay on the sun bed, slipped on her sunglasses and closed her eyes.

There were dresses and skirts and tops as well as a multi-collection of shorts in the closet and so she had told the driver, when he arrived, she did not wish to go to the mall. He seemed doubtful at her refusal, but with a shrug of his shoulders he went away. There was nothing appealing for her in the idea of going around a mall; she still felt out of sorts... it was ridiculous. The flight had been nothing out of the ordinary and not too long at that, yet she was feeling as if she had travelled to Australia and back again without a stopover.

Perhaps, she mused, it was all to do with how she felt about things. It was a kind of mental exhaustion rather than physical. That would hardly be surprising. After all, she was hardly having a wonderful time. The prospect of tomorrow at her mother-in-law's home filled her with dread. Not only had she probably to face Mercedes once more, but of more import, Michael's devious sister. It would be doubly hard to keep quiet, even though she knew she must. In one way, she hoped she had caught a virus and one that would prevent her from going. Knowing she was no coward was no consolation. She just did not feel up to acting out the charade.

She must have dozed, for she awoke with a start when she heard a door slam. Swinging her legs down from the sun bed she turned around. It was Michael striding purposefully towards her. He did not look pleased. In fact, she realised with a sinking feeling, he was looking really angry.

"Why do you never do anything you're asked to do?" he demanded when he reached her.

"Sorry?" she slipped her sunglasses to the top of her head, gazing up at him. The sun was behind her so she could see him clearly.

"I sent my driver to take you to the mall, but milady does not want to go; milady would rather soak up some sun by the pool."

"I didn't think it was a command," she said, managing to speak coldly. She swung her legs back onto the bed and stretched out. "And I didn't feel like it," she added.

"So what do you propose to wear tomorrow?" he asked. His eyes ran over her and she wished the sarong covered her upper body because the bikini top was far too revealing, barely cupping her high, full breasts.

"I have the suit I came in if it's formal, and if it isn't formal there are dresses in the closet. For goodness sake, you didn't tell me I needed a ball gown."

As she watched, he pulled off his jacket, casually throwing it onto the table behind them, then his tie and then he peeled off his silk shirt. Her mouth opened as he kicked off his shoes and pulled off his socks and then loosed his trousers. "What are you doing?" she asked.

"I hope I'm going to cool off," he said, "or I might say something I regret."

Quickly she slid her sunglasses onto her nose and looked away, only looking in the direction of the pool when she heard a splash. His shirt, underpants and socks were on the floor by the side of the sun bed. Sighing, she stood and, gathering them up, placed them on the table before going to the cabana and taking out a beach towel.

Michael was swimming furiously along the length of the pool. She sat at the edge and dipped her feet in the water, holding onto the towel with which she hoped he would maintain his modesty. If he had ever had any, she thought wryly.

Eventually after dozens of lengths, he swam to where she was. Leaning against the pool side, he rested his elbows on the tiles and glanced up at her.

"I didn't feel like going to a mall," she said, "I'm sorry, I thought people didn't go formal in Florida."

"People don't," he said, "but not at my Mom's on Thanksgiving. A sun dress? No way. We will have to go to the mall, or maybe I'll have the mall come here. Would you get my cell from my pocket, please?"

Only in America, she thought, as he punched in some numbers then spoke to someone, using all his charm and ordering a selection of outfits to be brought to the house. Apparently from what she heard they would come at seven.

He put the phone on the tiles. "Come in," he said, "it's good."

"I've been in," she said, more conscious of taking off the sarong than of being doubtful about going into the pool. The water looked so cool and inviting. Michael swam away; quickly she untied the sarong and slid into the water. Moving easily through the pool relaxed her. She had got a little warm from sitting in the sun and the water felt really good. Now she moved leisurely and not as if she was in a swimming race.

He swam to her and asked her if she liked it... the house, the pool, the climate...she answered in the affirmative. She was enthused about the house and the trees in the fields beyond the houses, the rolling gentle meadows, it was perfect.

When he swam to the steps, she gave him time to leave and wrap himself in the towel; it was stupid to feel that way. She knew that. After all, she had seen him without clothes many times, yet somehow this was different after the last time they had come together, and the way he had purposely made certain it would not happen again. He had become too distant from her to see him as Michael, her husband and her lover. He was the man she loved yet he was a stranger in some ways.

She swam to the steps and pulled herself out, looked for her sarong and saw it was gone. In a panic she looked around for it, saw Michael. He had it in his hands.

He held it out saying. "Come and get it."

"What are you doing?"

"A man has a right look at his wife and in that ... whew! Don't ever wear that in mixed company."

"I don't intend to." There was something hot in his gaze; he was feasting his eyes on her and she felt herself flush all over.

"Catch," he said.

She held out her hands and caught the sarong, then quickly fastened it around her, head down as she tied the strings.

"Satisfied?" he asked.

"About what?"

"Doing what you do," he murmured the statement.

"And what is that?" she asked, genuinely puzzled.

"Looking deliciously... "

"Deliciously what? I sense a criticism there."

"None intended. Let's say deliciously tempting." He turned away from her. "But let's not go there, it isn't fair to you and it certainly isn't fair to me."

"Sorry, I wasn't doing it on purpose. These were the only things in the closet, or should I have worn nothing and upset your staff?"

"I don't give a damn about my staff. However, you did happen to choose the sexiest bikini and a white one at that."

"I give up. Nothing I ever do seems to please you. I don't know why we have to keep this up. You're never going to like me, Michael. You're always going to find fault in everything I do and an ulterior motive, too." With tremendous effort she kept her voice level, attempting to hide the tumultuous feelings charging around her.

"Charley..." he paused, as if mulling over what he wanted to say. "I wasn't finding fault, exactly."

"What's that supposed to mean?" she asked when she thought she knew anyway.

She looked up at him. His face was blank of expression; part of her knew it would not be to her good to go across to him, yet she found herself drawn to him, as if he had wrapped her in invisible ties and could pull her to him whenever he wanted.

He said, when she stood facing him, "I think you're a woman who gets under a man's skin. A woman who can, for a time, make him believe that only he exists for her but that's an illusion, isn't it? It never will be just one man, will it?"

She gasped, opened and closed her mouth and opened it again, feeling there was no air to be had. She felt herself panting as if she had been running, trying to catch her breath. Having wounded her, he turned on his heels and went back into the house. She stood for several moments, feeling a tremendous churning in her stomach... it took only seconds to realise it was a real feeling of nausea, overwhelming in its intensity. She ran into the nearby pool room where she knew there was a toilet and shower. The tiles were cold to her knees, sending a little shock wave through her system.

She had eaten only a slice of brown toast for breakfast and had a glass of fresh orange juice and later coffee but it seemed as if everything she had ever eaten came from her stomach. Later, feeling weak and trembling, she lay down on the cold tiles, closing her eyes until the vertigo that was still with her passed.

Someone was calling her, a high pitched voice. "Senora, Senora..." it had to be Consuela's niece, Carmen, the pretty girl who had worn a rather spiteful expression when she had brought her breakfast that morning. Charley had put it down to the girl having a crush on Michael; it was easy to see how that was possible. He was the kind of man many women would get a crush on until they got to know him, she thought bitterly, until they realised how mean and unforgiving he could be.

Not wanting the girl to see her, she struggled up from the floor and called out. "I'll be in shortly, Carmen."

"Senor says you are to come for lunch," the girl called back, with hardly a modicum of respect in her voice. She commanded as Michael had probably commanded her.

"I'll be there when I'm ready," Charley answered.

"But, Senora..." the girl began to insist, and by the sound of her voice was coming closer to the pool room.

"I said when I am ready, Carmen." It was hard to make herself sound imperious. The thought of lunch and food had her stomach churning again. The girl left and Charley once more waited to see if she would be sick but there was nothing on her stomach. She knew she had to make it to the house as Michael would only come out to see why she could not do this simple thing. At least that was what he would think, believing it more defiance or awkwardness on her part.

It was cool in the house and she felt cold as she sluggishly went upstairs and into their bedroom. There was an internal phone and she rang down to the kitchen. Thankfully the friendly Consuela answered. "Consuela, please tell my husband I won't be down for lunch. I don't feel too good."

"Oh, Senora," the woman said. "Shall I bring the doctor?"

"No, it's nothing; I'll be fine, thank you, Consuela."

"If you are sure."

"Quite sure, Consuela."

Putting down the phone she went and closed the shutters and turned off the hum of air conditioning, and, after taking a quick warm shower, she crawled into bed. Pulling the cover over her, she still felt chilled. A door opened, closing after only a moment. Her heart rose and dipped on a wave of fear and anticipation but Michael, for she was sure it was he, must have decided to let her rest.

She slept deep and long and was only awakened by someone's gentle tapping on the door. She struggled out of the comforter and realised she was very warm now but also that she felt hungry and rested. To her "come in," Consuela came carrying a tray of tea things.

"Oh, thank you!" she murmured. It was just what she needed. There was a honey cake on the tray and checking her watch she saw it was four o'clock; she had slept for about four hours.

"Senor say maybe you would like this tea and my little honey cakes. How are you, Senora?"

"Much better, thank you, Consuela."

"Shall I open the shutters?"

"Please do."

When the woman had gone, Charley left the bed and went to the bathroom for a silk robe. After tying it securely, she went and poured the tea and took up the honey cake. The pastry was delicious and the tea refreshing. A slight breeze disturbed the bed hangings; it was warm but not so warm she should put the cooler back on.

She took the tea things over to the occasional table and sat in the comfortable chair pondering over what had happened to her. She was not constitutionally a sickly person, yet these past few days she had felt more weak and sickly than she had felt in years. She knew it was not the change in climate. A thing like that never bothered her and besides, the weather in Florida just then was not sticky hot but a wonderfully Mediterranean type of heat she was used to.

The door opened and Michael came through it. She turned away from him. In a white polo shirt and shorts, bare footed and with his hair casual, he looked so attractive. He could wear anything and look good, but in casual gear he looked dangerously approachable. However, she knew he was the same animal no matter what the clothing.

"How are you?" he asked. She glanced at him; he had his hands in his pockets, elbows akimbo as if he was afraid he would touch her.

"Better, thanks," she murmured, taking up her cup of tea and sipping it, hoping it would give her strength and confidence. "Thank you for having them bring this. It was just what I needed."

"What's the problem? Too much sun do you think?"

"Probably, I don't really know, but I'm fine now. Really, no need to panic."

"Do you think you will be okay for tomorrow?" he asked gently.

That did it. His compassion proven false she put down her cup and jumped out of the chair. Facing him, she clenched her hands tightly. "Oh no, I must not inconvenience you and your plans, whatever else might be happening. If I was dying on my feet you'd expect me to fulfil my duties. And don't worry, Michael, I will, but I tell you this, this is the last time. I'm finished now, and you can go to hell in a handcart for all I care. You can stick your money, your influence, whatever. I think I'd rather go bankrupt than have any more to do with this."

The silence hung between them, the only sound the slight wind whispering against the screens.

He pulled his hands out of his pockets. One hand went up to the pocket on his polo shirt; he pulled something out which he tossed on the table.

"Your air ticket to England. You leave on the second of December."

With that he turned and left, quietly closing the door behind him. She felt her eyes burn with tears and yet why should she cry? She had what she wanted.

She picked up the ticket; it was first class from Tampa to New York. There was a stopover, presumably for her to collect her things at the apartment, and then she was to leave the following day, the third of December.

The second leg of the journey was by first class also. Then why was she crying? But she knew it was the way he had done it. The contemptuous look he gave to her, the way his mouth twisted in a cynical expression.

He really despised her. Nothing that had happened had altered anything and it hurt too, to realise he did not know her at all, had not gauged in their closeness she was not the person he thought her to be. So much for his astuteness where people were concerned, yet she had to concede, whatever did being astute have to do with matters of the heart?

Six

The dress she had chosen made her feel really good about herself. It was a thin crepe in green and gold, fitted at the waist with a draped skirt that had a split to the knee to one side. The bodice was cross over, fitted at her breasts, but it was both sophisticated and respectable. Having washed and restyled her hair herself, it hung in a curved arch at her chin and neck and had a high shine. There was no need for foundation since her skin was very lightly toasted, but she added a cheerful pink lipstick and slicked just a modicum of blusher on her cheeks.

Michael drove to his mother's home which was close to the beach, a large elegant white house set in half an acre of grounds. There was a lake and trees and beyond a fairly new golf course. Michael told her his father had had the golf course built. It had given him somewhere to go when he retired. Now his mother received a considerable income from the club. Whether by purpose or accident, they were the last to arrive and the rest of the company was assembled on the covered terrace at the back of the house.

The lunch was a catered affair, Michael informed her. His mother always gave her staff the day off for Thanksgiving so they could visit their own families.

Charley tilted her chin as they were guided through by a white-coated waiter. There was a lot of chatter. They could hear it as they approached, but it was immediately cut off when they stepped out onto the terrace. The silence was quite potent and she was glad to feel Michael's arm slide around her waist. As it was, she felt the hot blush sliding up her neck and to her cheeks. She was the centre for all eyes and she felt as if she were a specimen in a laboratory.

A tall, good looking man stepped forward. He was very distinguished-looking and with that dark Spanish attractiveness Michael had. He held out his hand. "Charley, I'm so pleased to meet you at last." He took hold of her hand warmly and held it no longer than it would be polite to do so.

Michael said. "This is Joe, Charley." He hesitated. "My big brother."

She turned to look at Michael; she had not known he had a brother, let alone an older one. She wondered why it was he ran the company himself and why Joe had nothing to do with it. At least she had never heard of a Joe being in the company.

"Hello," and because she was shy and still confused, she added, "I didn't know there was a Joe."

He smiled down into her eyes, his eyes wrinkling at the corners. He was very handsome. She saw in him a glimpse of how Michael would age. "But I knew there was a Charley!"

A woman, blonde and pretty, came to his side. She was petite, fairy light and delicately boned. She looked at Charley directly and put out her hand, too. "I'm Anna, the wife..." she smiled, a warm smile that engulfed Charley. "And it's lovely to meet you after all this time."

The thing she noticed was Anna was not Spanish. She was a blue eyed, very pale skinned blonde. The fact intrigued Charley, especially after what Mrs Hernandez had specifically told Charley that Charley would not fit in because she was not, in Michael's mother's opinion, from the right culture.

Michael's mother came then, kissing Michael on both cheeks and merely welcoming Charley with brief touch of her hand. A waiter came with drinks; Charley felt her stomach revolt at the smell of the wine and asked instead for a sparkling water. As he was driving, Michael asked for the same.

Quickly, as she took hold of the chilled tall crystal glass tinkling with ice cubes, she scanned the other guests. Nowhere did she see Mercedes or her father. There were two older people, to whom she was being steered, and, sitting on the silk covered sofa close by, a younger woman whom she recognised as Maria. However, it was a Maria who was older and plumper. By her side a man with blue-black hair and a slim moustache. He looked, Charley thought, with a tickle of humour, rather like a matinee idol from a thirties film.

The older couple were Yolanda Hernandez's sister and her husband. They were all making polite conversation when a young girl came up to them. She was a good looking girl but Charley sensed one who was, at that time, unhappy in her skin. She looked as if she would prefer to be miles away from the gathering and out of the little black dress she was wearing. Although the dress suited her slender figure, she gave the appearance of being uncomfortable, by constantly tugging at the round neck. It was obviously not a dress she particularly liked.

"Hi," she said to no one in particular.

She glanced at Michael and following her gaze, Charley saw Michael frowning down at the girl.

"Aunt, Uncle." She acknowledged the couple, nodding her head. "Charlotte," she added. Her huge brown eyes poured over Charley, making her feel a little uncomfortable. She was about eighteen.

"Charley, this is Dolores, my youngest sister, who seems to have left her manners elsewhere."

"Hello, Dolores," Charley said, extending her hand. The younger girl seemed to hesitate. Michael gave his sister the lightest of pushes and the girl took hold of Charley's hand, giving it a brief but firm shake. The aunt and uncle moved away with a polite nod in Charley's direction, and a rather disapproving look at Dolores.

"I believe you're at college here. What are you studying?"

"Languages," the girl said.

"That sounds interesting."

"It isn't really; I wanted to do something else."

"What was that?"

Michael said. "She wanted to study the hotel business."

"Oh, really? Yet you chose languages because…"

"Because I was good at it and because Michael wanted me to," she said sulkily.

138

Or, Charley wondered, ordered you to? She looked at Michael, a question in her eye, but he moved away, leaving Charley alone with the discontented girl.

"You know, I don't know why you're back in Michael's life... after the last time."

"I'm sorry?"

"You broke his heart!" The girl spoke with the unbridled honesty of the young, her large chocolate coloured eyes practically giving out sparks.

Charley gasped, not only astonished at the vehement way the girl spoke but because somehow she knew it was partly true. She did not believe it was quite as dramatic as that, for he had not loved her deeply enough to pursue her. However, Charley had come to realise Michael had been hurt by her, as he saw it, betrayal. It was something she had known for some time. That was the only reason for his caution as far as she was concerned. He never wanted to be hurt again. He would go so far and then no further. Sex was obviously all right, some of the time, but commitment was never going to be in the cards.

Obviously, no one had shared the truth with Dolores. She did not know of her older sister machinations or the fact that she, Charley, had believed Michael had broken her heart!

"I would never forgive anyone who did that to me," Dolores spoke with passion.

"While I respect your opinion of me, Dolores, it really is between Michael and me."

"I love my brother. He is everything to me."

"Then you would want his happiness, I'm sure."

Dolores thought about it for a moment, tugging at the neckline of her dress and giving herself a little shake like a flea ridden dog.

Charley felt no animosity towards the girl, in spite of what she had said. She could see her for what she was; a young and insecure girl, just at that time in her life unhappy with herself for some reason or other.

"Why don't you change out of that dress?" Charley said kindly. "I can see you don't like it."

"I hate it. I hate dresses but my mother would have apoplexy if I wore what I wanted."

"You must have another dress."

"It's even more uncomfortable."

"You have only one other dress?"

"No, of course I don't."

"Why don't we go and look through your wardrobe to see what we can come up with."

"I don't want you to be my friend," the girl snapped back.

"Okay, but that doesn't devalue my opinion, does it?"

"I guess not. Come on, then, but there isn't anything remotely suitable."

Dolores had a large bedroom filled with books but remarkably tidy for a teenager. She admitted the maid did a good job when Charley complimented her.

In the walk in closet, Charley could see what Dolores meant. There were piles of t-shirts and sweaters and there had to be a hundred pairs of pants and jeans. There were only four dresses. One was a dark amber silk with a v-neck and a tie belt. It looked cool and comfortable and Charley lifted it from the rail, holding it against her.

"There's nothing wrong with this," she suggested.

"I wore it last year," Dolores said sulkily.

"So, do you want to be comfortable or not? And who do you think will remember what you wore?"

"My mother will notice."

"But she would want you to be comfortable. How will you enjoy your Thanksgiving dinner if you are wriggling all over the place and tugging at that neck? I can see it's already out of shape. Your skin's a little red from your tugging it. Put this on."

Dolores hesitated then took up the dress. "Okay. Will you wait outside, please?"

"Of course."

When she came out she looked much better; there was no neckline for her to tug at and the dress fit her slender figure perfectly. It was far more flattering to her than the little black dress had been.

"You look lovely," Charley said.

"I feel better. But no one looks as gorgeous as you." As a compliment it was said in a most disagreeable way so Charley hardly felt flattered. It was almost an accusation.

"Why didn't you do the hotel course at college?"

"Michael figured I should learn the business from him. He believes languages would be good because one day I could take over the running of hotels out of the States. He's right, of course. No one else is interested in the business but me, and he needs someone to help him."

"That would be good for you both. What an exciting life you can have!"

"Maybe, but I might just get married, who knows?" she said with a shrug.

"Play it by ear," Charley counselled. "You never know what's around the corner. Anyway, even if you marry, languages will always enable you to make a decent living and have a career."

"I don't need to make a living. I have a trust fund," she said.

"Oh, lucky you," Charley murmured.

The girl looked down at her feet, then when she looked up at Charley,

Charley saw that her large, soft brown eyes were full of confusion.

"I don't know what I want," the girl admitted.

Charley thought when she was eighteen... back in England nursing a broken heart but having, for financial reasons, to pull herself together. She had had to work and take her training in day release. She had done all kinds of jobs, from chambermaid to kitchen porter. Only in the darkness of night when she lay in her solitary bed did she have time to indulge her pain. Yet she could sympathise so easily with Dolores Hernandez. She knew about how difficult it was to be young and not to know where you wanted to head, how your body could play havoc with the hormonal balance.

"It will work out, Dolores, you'll see. Michael said you've only just started at college, so I'll bet you've found that fairly confusing."

"I have," the girl admitted. "Everyone seems to run in a crowd, and I just don't fit in."

"Tell me about it," she said kindly.

"We'd better go. We can still talk if you like."

Dolores poured out all her confusion as they went back to where the others were. Dolores not fitting in was due to her mother being so strict. She had not even joined a sorority because her mother did not approve. Dolores was wishing she had gone to college out of state, but she had been talked into staying at home by her mother. That also put her a little out of things because many of the students had come from out of state. Even those students who were local to the college had more freedom than she enjoyed.

"Maybe Michael can help you, Dolores; he isn't an ogre, you know."

"I know he would but he has been so busy and everything and what with you coming back into his life. You've taken up all his time."

If only, Charley thought, knowing that was never going to be true. "Would you like me to talk to him about it?"

"Would you?" The girl's face was eager now, and it was so easy for Charley to make her a promise. Besides, she was sure that Michael had influence with his mother, more so than anyone else.

"I don't suppose Joe would help as well?" she asked.

"Oh no, Joe has his own problems with Mom. But Michael has a lot of influence with her."

The inevitable came and it was Michael who came to her and said he would introduce her to his sister Maria. He escorted her over to where Maria and her husband were sitting. He stood, but Maria remained seated. It was when she drew closer she saw Maria was heavily pregnant.

"My sister, Maria and her husband, Ramon. Maria as you can see is almost due to make my mother a grandmother."

"Michael," Maria said but not without humour. "Welcome, Charley," she added and her smile seemed a little nervous.

"Thank you."

"But he never told us how beautiful you are," Ramon added.

"Of course I didn't! I would not let you know that above anyone!"

Glancing at him, she saw her husband's eyes had narrowed and Maria was looking at her brother with some kind of desperate plea in her eyes.

A waiter came with a tray of huge shrimp and other titbits but Charley did not take any, in spite of the urgings of Michael that she try at least one shrimp and the chilli sauce with it.

"No really, I'd rather not," she said. She took a long sip of water.

Maria said. "I usually love them but I must be careful of seafood with the baby and everything."

Glad of a let out, Charley asked. "When is your baby due, Maria?"

"January," she said and smiled. It was hard to reconcile this heavily pregnant woman with the spiteful girl who had come to the flat in New Rochelle. That was eight years ago and Maria had to have been about eighteen. Now she was in her twenties and there was something rather old fashioned about her... it was in her hair style and her dress sense.

Ramon said. "Sit here, Charley, you and Maria must have so much in common."

There was something so sarcastic in the comment, she saw Michael throw him a suspicious and rather unpleasant look. Charley had been on the end of that look and she had not liked it one bit. Contrarily, Ramon merely sauntered off, hardly disturbed by the antipathy so obviously displayed towards him by his brother-in-law. Thinking it wisest, Charley took the seat Ramon had vacated.

Michael seeing them as he imagined settle together, wandered off to speak with his brother and his wife.

"Thank you," Maria said, "for your discretion," she added in case Charley had not understood her meaning.

A caustic comment or two came into Charley's mind, but she disregarded them. Looking at Maria now she knew she could not say anything nasty. The woman was obviously suffering in the later stages of her pregnancy. Her feet were slightly swollen and her belly looked as if it were holding more than one baby.

"It's over with now. How come Mercedes did not come, or is she coming later?"

"She's not; she finally has the message. Her father and she have gone on holiday. I think she's desperate now to find a husband. She feels really humiliated," the girl stopped then said quietly, "and so she should be."

Kettles and pots came to mind, but again Charley decided to say nothing. "It's a relief not to have to face her again."

"You did all right last time," Maria said. "My mother told me all about it. She was quite surprised at the way you handled yourself."

"So…" Charley began, wanting to change the subject. "Michael tells me you now live in Mexico?"

Maria seized on the lifeline and talked of where she lived, how long she had been married and how this baby had been a long time being conceived. There had been many years of agony and tests and, in the end, they had thought they would never have a child.

They had not considered IVF; it was something Ramon would not even consider. In fact, Maria confessed, she was certain he would sooner divorce her and remarry than have a child that way, which Charley considered both hurtful and selfish. However, against all the odds Maria had conceived, and just at that time when she had believed it would never happen.

Any bitterness fled from Charley as she heard the sad story. She could not even dream anymore of taking revenge on this girl. Life had been somewhat unkind to her as it was, and anyway, there was no point in causing upheaval. The day after tomorrow she would be on her way back to her old life, this sorry experience put behind her. Michael and his bitterness would be gone forever. She would survive it all; she was like that, a survivor. Nothing could be as devastating as the last time she had left. That pain had seared her very soul; nothing could ever be as bad as that again.

Lunch was announced and Michael came to claim her again. He took her arm as if she were the most precious thing in his life. If only, she thought, that was real. It was odd to realise she did not feel uncomfortable with his family. In fact, the reverse was true, she felt quite relaxed about them. They were not the threatening tribe of her imagination. Even the distance his mother kept was in some ways forgivable. The matriarch would never truly warm to her, but if it were all for real and not a façade, then that would not matter either. It was the way Senora Hernandez was, and there was nothing Charley could ever do to change her.

Thankfully, she saw she was sitting opposite Joe and Anna. Michael and his mother were at opposite ends of the table at the head, Charley at his right and the aunt was next to her. She thought it odd Michael's elder brother was not at the head of the table but he did not seem to resent that he was sidelined by his younger brother.

The first course was a crisp salad. Ravenous now, Charley really enjoyed it. She took only water and refused the wine, turning her wine glass down so that none could be poured into it. Michael said, in merely a murmur. "Have some wine; don't worry that I'm not drinking."

"I'm fine, I… after yesterday… I don't feel like any."

"Yesterday?" His eyes narrowed. "What yesterday? You were tired, isn't that all?"

She blushed, thinking of how it had been for her in the pool room. "I… I think it was a chill on my tummy, best not to encourage any further turbulence."

He raised an eyebrow imperiously, then turned to Anna and said something she could not hear. Anna gave a schoolgirl giggle so Charley was relieved it obviously was not anything to do with her.

The turkey was moist and delicious, and there were creamed squash and new and roast potatoes, cranberry sauce and fresh green beans. The whole feast was a wonderful treat for Charley, who could not remember when she had last had a traditional meal.

At Christmas time, she was usually working flat out and the last thing she wanted when she arrived home was a turkey dinner, having been around turkey dinners for weeks in the hotel business. This, though, was different. She enjoyed the atmosphere and the meal and was touched that Michael had led a prayer before they ate. She thought it a wonderful occasion to celebrate.

There was pumpkin pie for dessert and she took the tiniest slice the waiter could manage to cut.

During the meal she learned much about Joe. He had not wanted to be in the family business and had gone his own way. He was a cancer specialist in Tampa. He had met Anna when he was an intern and she had been a nurse. "That went down like a fox in a hen house, I can tell you. The eldest son, marrying out, I mean not only was dear Anna not Spanish, she was not even a Catholic. I think it was three years before anyone spoke to me."

"That's terrible," Charley said.

"Dad was a real stickler for tradition. The old lady's learning; give her time," he winked.

"She's much better now," Anna piped up. "We get along fine, although I'm still kept at a little distance because I have not produced the offspring. I wanted to go to med school myself and train as a doctor. I finish this year, finally, and then I might have a child, if I can persuade my husband," she grinned, gazing up at Joe.

He covered her delicate hand in his large one. "Whatever you want, honey." They were so obviously in love it made her ache and Joe was so natural, open and different. No one had succeeded in repressing him, she saw. He had courageously done his own thing and hang the consequences.

"Anyway, the pressure should be off now that Maria is going to do the decent thing," Joe laughed. "Though I hope it has more of its mother than its father."

"Joe," Anna cautioned, glancing down the table. A laugh rumbled from him and Charley compressed her mouth so she, too, did not laugh. She rather thought Joe in his observation was right. There was something just a little creepy and oily about Ramon.

"Coffee is on the terrace," Senora Hernandez announced. Michael came behind Charley and politely moved her chair for her to leave the table as she stood.

As the afternoon progressed, Charley found it so easy to talk to Joe and Anna. Here she found companions she could get along with. They seemed to be on her wave length and there was no awkwardness. As she was leaving, Anna said she and Michael must come and visit them for dinner one evening. Charley realised, with a jolt, she would not see them again. She hesitated, unsure what to say. Then she decided on the truth. "I'm going back to England the day after tomorrow."

"Perhaps when you come back, we can have such fun," Anna said. "And now I've finished my training, we can meet during the day." She giggled a little mischievously. "At last I've a sister-in-law I can relate to." Then in a confiding tone she added. "I used to live in dread that Mercedes Mendoza would get her way. I'm so happy Michael has found you again."

Charley felt sick at the words, hated herself for the deceit. Somehow deceiving the open and friendly Joe and Anna seemed far worse than the other members of the family, who had, albeit politely, kept her at a distance.

"Let me have your address. I'll write to you," Charley said quickly.

"Michael has it," Joe said. "Mike and I have never been estranged. He's a great guy, you know. I think you're both lucky."

The great guy was at her side. He put a hand to her elbow firmly. "We have to go now," he said.

"Oh, must we?" Charley said. "I was really enjoying myself."

"So I see. Joe, I'm going to take Charley around to say goodbye to everyone, then we have to leave. I'll give you a call next time I'm down."

"Do that, Mike; we can all get together."

"Sure," Michael said, showing no sign whatsoever that this was never going to happen, at least not with Charley at his side.

Saying goodbye to the others was quite formal, although Senora Hernandez managed to peck Charley on the cheek. "No doubt I will see you soon, Charlotte," the older woman said. Then there were Maria and her husband. Maria stood wearily and took up Charley's hand briefly. "It has been a pleasure to meet you," she said.

"Thank you, I hope everything goes great for you," Charley said and she meant it.

~ * ~

Michael said, as he ploughed the car through the traffic. "Thank God that's over."

"I thought it a nice afternoon."

"Yes, my brother and his wife are good company."

"The food was wonderful. I think it's a lovely idea, Thanksgiving. It's special somehow."

"It can be," Michael murmured. "Usually, but there have been times when it has been nothing more than a duty."

"Like Christmas Day," she said. "My mother always used to get in such a spin on Christmas Day; I used to think it wasn't worth all the fuss. I like the idea of Christmas... it's just the actual that can be a pain."

"You never talk about your mother. I think that's the first time she's ever come into any conversation I've had with you. How is she? I never got to meet her, first time around or second, it seems."

"She married again. My stepfather died and out in Arizona where she was living, she met an Englishman. They married and for some reason or other, they went to live back in Europe. They have a place in southern Spain. She's happy. I seldom go to see them, and they don't seem to care."

"I always got the impression she was pretty selfish," Michael said.

"Well..." she hesitated, not wanting to exchange these kinds of things with him. "A bit, I suppose. She was an adored only child, so I think she was a little spoilt. It's okay. I'm not bitter or anything about it. In fact, we get on better when we just talk on the phone than when we are together. I think I remind her too much of my father."

"That's no bad thing. I really liked your dad."

"I'm glad," she said feeling a sudden warm glow. Charles Bloom had been a lovely man, and she felt sad that she had not had long enough with him.

"Michael, I had a long chat with Dolores."

"Yeah, I saw that. Say what did you do to get her out of that funereal outfit she was wearing... and wearing it as if it were a hair shirt?"

"With a little friendly persuasion. She was telling me about college. Michael, do you think you could help her?"

He listened carefully, nodding now and again, not taking his eyes from the road, or his hands from the wheel, but he was paying attention to what she was telling him.

"I'm on to it," he said when she finished. "And I'm glad you got her to open up. I thought she seemed a bit down. Dolores can be a pain in the butt, but there's something good about her, too. I was never around much when she was growing but in some ways she's the one person in the family who is most like me. Maria is my mother's child, that's for sure and as for Joe... who knows who Joe takes after, some throwback from way back, I guess." He laughed softly. "Joe was so rebellious you know, I always thought of him as my hero. But he wasn't a rebel without a cause; he knew what he wanted, and he went out and got it. I admire that about people. I can get my mother off Dolores' back and give her some slack. The kid has to have a good college experience; otherwise, there is no point to her being there."

They drove the rest of the way in silence. When they reached the house, Michael drove directly into the garage after dropping her off at the front door. It was very quiet and cool in the house. Consuela had left some cold cuts in the refrigerator in case they needed to eat. The sun was casting long golden beams across the lanai so she went out there after collecting a book she was reading.

Concentration eluded her. She put the book down and just gazed out over the pool. In a little while, Michael came wearing a pair of white swimming shorts. He dived in the pool. She thought it would be fun to join him but refrained from moving. She would have to go to her room, put on one of the swimsuits, which would probably result in some kind of sarcasm from Michael. They were all so brief, so she did not want to be accused of trying to tempt him.

It was very still and quiet; the only sound was rushing water as Michael swam backwards and forwards. Then even that stopped and he was there, in front of her, dripping water on the tiles. His body, well muscled, was quite tanned but as he reached for a towel, there was a lighter ridge of skin revealed which had not been exposed to the sun. The shorts clung to his hips, flattened against his muscular thighs. They, being white, revealed his flesh through the material. He had turned his back to her and had his arms outstretched as he wiped the wetness from his arms. She watched the muscles of his back ripple with the movement and longed to just go and run her nails along that taut bronzed flesh.

Her whole body ached from longing for him, each sensitised nerve tugging and teasing, and the pert peaks of her breasts thrust forward. Nervously she just ran her fingers across them, hardly surprised to find they felt so hard. Warm moisture pooled at her thighs. He was not even touching her, or even looking at her, yet her body was ready for his. It was shocking to discover that no matter how cold he was towards her, she would ever be warm with longing for the ultimate consummation.

Unsteadily, she swung her legs onto the tiles, pulled herself up and then walked back into the house; forcing herself to walk steadily and not to sway and sashay when that was all she really wanted to do.

Once in her room, she took a long cold shower, and after found some casual slacks and a top to wear. Instead of going downstairs she went and sat on the balcony. Picking up her book again, she forced herself to read but soon realised the words were making no inroads into her mind. Misery swamped her, draining the last vestiges of energy. Perhaps, she consoled herself with the thought, when she arrived back in England and had to start to deal with the hotel business, then she would feel better. She would be really busy and that was the best thing of all to mend a broken heart.

A movement behind her disturbed her thoughts. Turning, she saw Michael standing just inside the door frame looking at her, a towel around his middle.

She left her chair and went in through the louvered doors. "Did you want me?" she asked, trying to sound normal.

"Like crazy," he said.

"I'm sorry?"

"So am I," he said as he moved towards her. She thought she should move back, to get away, knowing it would be unbearable to be in his arms, but so right, too. She stood poised, waiting till he reached her.

He seized her hair, not hurting her although his grip was firm. His eyes were all over her face, drinking in the wide golden eyes, the perfectly formed nose, her lips, full and round and as he gazed at them, parting, her tongue, pink and delicious, moving slowly across her teeth in a gesture that had more to do with nerves than seduction.

Her hands, limp at her sides, moved in slow motion Finally finding the hard muscled flesh of his back, she slid her hands down the taut flesh. Her eyes, she remembered with a shiver, had pored over him downstairs, and she had longed with mad voyeuristic pleasure to do just this.

As she moved her lower body against his, she could feel through the thickness of the towel his pulsating need of her. In a gesture of insane joy, she tossed back her head, exposing the perfect line of her throat. He bent his head, kissing the column very gently, before lazily stroking it with his tongue, until he reached her ear. His teeth captured the tiny lobe before his tongue moved over the crevice in warm stroking movements that set her blood on fire.

When his lips at last captured hers, she melded herself against him, with such ferocity the towel at his middle loosened and whispered to his feet. Eagerly she ran her hands down him, caressing the length of his spine, cupping the round hard flesh of his bottom.

His hands were inside the thin tee shirt, then down into the waistband of her lightweight pants, easing them off her hips, exposing her burning flesh and letting her feel hard against her warm moist centre, his maleness.

He lifted her up against him, shaking the trousers from her feet, disentangling her from them, raising her arms and pulling her free from the tee shirt. His hands cupped and tenderly caressed her breasts, his mouth capturing the pouting peak, suckling the centre until it was wet and hard before swinging her up in his arms and carrying her to the bed. Michael lay her down gently, kneeling over her, his mouth capturing hers while his hands played down the length of her thrashing body. Finding her core, he tenderly plunged his finger into the gushing liquid of her, felt her nails at his back, her teeth against his devouring mouth. Eagerly he tore his mouth from hers, travelling her body with hot sweet damp kisses… going down her, beyond the moist curls and along the pink petal of her femininity.

She cried out; his name a sob on her mouth.

He moved, slowly, deliberately, taking her lips once more, and then lunged himself into her, feeling the hot glorious agony of her staining him. Locked together, they slid from the now, feeling the passion envelop and drive them ever onwards into an ecstasy of feeling that was electrifying in its intensity.

Seven

She awoke to see Michael, head propped on hand, elbow bent, looking down at her. For a moment she held his gaze before her lids fluttered closed, the long thick lashes casting shadows on her cheeks. He traced a finger down her face, from eyebrow to rim, as if he were drawing her. She opened her eyes; he was still there, watching her, his eyes intense in their scrutiny of her.

"What is it?" she asked.

"Nothing, just looking… you look as if butter wouldn't melt in your mouth, do you know that?"

"No, I didn't know that," she said softly.

"Especially when you're sleeping. You know, no woman does to me what you do."

"They don't?"

"No…"

"And what is that exactly?" she asked, feeling good about herself, enjoying the tingling feeling of vanity his words awakened inside her.

"It's… like, when I've made love with you, then I want to do it again, and I could, you know. It's sort of like when you're scared, and yet you're thrilled so that when you stop doing the scary thing, you just want to do it over."

She laughed softly. "I'm not sure whether to be flattered or not."

"Believe me, be flattered. How about you?"

"Me?"

She moved a little, feeling uncomfortable, aware of her cheeks staining red.

"You, how do you feel with me?"

What to say? The truth was that there never had been any other guys, but wouldn't that reveal too much about her? It would let him know for certain she had never gotten over him.

When in doubt, she thought prevarication was the best method of defence. "Come on, Michael don't tell me you need your ego stroked."

"No, I don't need that."

He moved his hand into the silk coverlet, finding her waist and resting there, his fingers spread. "What are you going to do with the rest of your life?" he asked again.

"Be happy."

"Not successful?"

"Don't the two go hand in hand?"

"Not necessarily. Tell me, how will you achieve that?"

"By making Bloom's a success," she lied. How could she say her true happiness would be found by being with him, and just that? If it was all real, if there was something inside him that could really love her again, deeply, truly and forever, then that would be enough. That it would be just the two of them, caring for each other and nothing else would ever matter.

"You can do that now, everything's in place, so when you go back you can start in. I'd be interested to see how it goes."

Now she had it, absolute proof. He had been putting things in hand, organising his half of the deal, making it good. She had to have played her part well. As to this, being this close, she looked up at him... his eyes were narrowed a little and he was weighing her very carefully, watching her face so intently she was certain the thoughts that fluttered through her mind were there for him to read. She had to pull back; he must never know she loved him. Perhaps it would give him a perverse kind of pleasure to know that. It could be his ultimate revenge. He was walking away leaving her in pain as she had left him, or so he believed.

"It'll be a challenge," she said.

"But you will do it?"

"I hope so."

He lay down, his hands now behind his head; he was staring up at the ceiling as if it were really interesting. With curled fingers, she cupped a muscle on his upper arm, liking the strong feel of it, and then moved her fingers down into the warmth beneath his arm, enjoying the feel of silky dark hair beneath her questing fingers. "That used to tickle like hell," he said, his voice husky at the edges.

"And now...?" She moved her hand ever so gently into the pit of his arm.

"Sort of, but not in the way that makes me laugh."

She rose over him, smoothing her hand over his chest, then bending her head and taking his lips very lightly between her teeth, sliding her tongue inside his mouth, until with a gasp of pleasure, he slid his arms around her, caressing the length of her back.

Charley very slowly placed her legs over his, bringing herself over him, while her mouth continued to devour his. She stretched herself along the length of him, feeling him come to life against her. She realised this would probably be the last time she could be like this with him, that he would be gone when she left for New York. In the drowsy aftermath of their lovemaking, he had said he had to go to Miami and then on to the Caribbean on business for a couple of days. He had not said he would not see her again, but she knew that was what would happen. Her ticket home was in her bag.

He felt her hesitation, raised her head, his hand lost in her thick hair, his eyes looking deeply into hers.

"Charlotte?" he asked huskily. In reply she raised herself over him, and then as she slid him inside her, his mouth parted and he gasped in surprise at the suddenness of her movement. "Oh, baby…" he said, sliding his arms around her, running the palms down her back, and cupping the round fullness of her hips. "Charlotte, baby…"

Then she lost herself, going with him to slide into that secret and all consuming ecstasy, tomorrow gone from her mind, conscious only of the now and this scorching fusion of their bodies.

~ * ~

Charley laid back in the tub, bubbles all around her, and the perfume intoxicating. She was feeling more relaxed than she had felt in months. Tired and yet oddly exhilarated. A rare combination of feeling that was pleasurable.

"Charley," the faintly deep husky voice penetrated her ear. She opened her eyes. Michael was sitting on the rim of the tub, fresh from his shower, wrapped in a pale blue towelling robe. "Why don't you come with me?"

"What?" She clutched the sponge to her, sinking lower in the bubbles, wetting the back of her hair. "To Miami, then to the Bahamas. It will be a kind of holiday for you."

"Michael, I have been on holiday," she smiled at him. "I have never been so lazy." Her heart was skipping and jumping all over the place. He wanted her to go with him, not to play games, not for any other purpose than he wanted her there at his side. She wanted to say yes straight away, yet caution held her back as well as common sense.

"You gave me a ticket home."

"So," he shrugged.

"And then there's the hotel," she said, being practical. "Surely I need to be there to…"

"Look, you know the schedule. Bob has his Christmas parties booked till the twenty-first of December, and then the hotel closes. The builders move in the second of January and move out the thirtieth of March. What can you do? Sit amongst a lot of rubble and dust?"

She looked at him; there was little expression on his face and yet she sensed something inside him, something he was not revealing to her.

"If you've got plans just say," he said and there was just the slightest hint of tension in his voice.

"I don't have any plans," she admitted. "But why do you want me to come with you?"

He shrugged again, dipping his hands into the water and bringing his hands up with a handful of bubbles in the palm, watching them, fascinated, as they melted away.

"Why not; we have fun, don't we?"

A tremor of disappointment passed over her. It was probably a very truthful answer. They did have fun but there was little else they shared. Had she imagined he would fall in love with her all over again? What they shared was a mutual passion; she could not expect anything else. She gazed over at him, surprised to see his eyes were on her, watching her and weighing, while at the same time he remained inscrutable.

Her pride took a beating; her common sense raged against the injustice of her decision.

"I'd really like that, Michael," she said.

He bent over her, capturing her lips in his, gently caressing them until they parted, then with a slight growl of regret, he slid his mouth from hers, pausing only to kiss the tip of her nose before he made to leave the bathroom. "I'll make the arrangements," he said. "Then I'll order breakfast. What would you like, honey?"

"Just that," she said with a smile, "on a little toast, of course."

~ * ~

Settled on the private jet, she felt a little feeling of fear feather over her; he must have seen it for he asked Col to bring her a glass of wine. When the steward brought the wine and she raised it to her lips, the scent of the wine opened up a tract of nausea in her stomach. It was crawling its way into the back of her throat. Putting the wine down, she headed for the bathroom.

The steady drum of the plane seemed louder in the bathroom. It did something to her ears that only increased the feeling of sickness. She managed to kneel over the toilet bowl before her stomach released the contents of her breakfast. The cold and hot waves of dizziness she had experienced in the pool room flooded over her again. Only this time, she felt cold sweat break out on her forehead and run down between her breasts. She felt as if she were going to pass out and let herself sink slowly to the floor. Here there was thick carpet and she laid her head against the pile, waiting for the dizzying waves to pass by.

Someone was knocking on the outer door. It was Michael, calling her name. She cried with effort: "I'm all right, really."

"Really? What the hell does that mean? I'm coming in," he said commandingly.

She cried out not to, but her cry was feeble and he probably did not hear her. She cursed not having locked the door; she just did not need him to see her like this. He would think her some kind of weakling and so needed him to see her as strong and fit.

"God, Charlotte, what in the hell..." he knelt at her side, putting out a hand to her forehead. She tried to struggle up but he held her fast. "Rest a minute," Michael ordered and in such a way that she complied. "I had no idea you suffered from air sickness to such an extent."

Neither did I, she thought, but she said nothing. He supported her head in his lap, pushing back the damp strands of hair from her face, then with one hand reaching up for a packet of wet wipes, struggling one free and very gently wiping her face with it.

"That feels good," she murmured. "I can get up now." He helped her, very slowly; she clasped an arm around his, and his other arm supported her waist. Her legs felt like a young foal's.

"Col has some good herbal recipe for this; you'd be amazed how many executives get sick on little jets."

"It's not that little," she said, managing a wan smile. "But I am glad I'm not on my own. I feel such a fool."

"Maybe you should lie down for a while," he suggested as they entered the corridor.

"You'd do anything to get me into bed," she looked up at him, "but I am sure I'll be better sitting up."

"I guess you can read my mind," he teased back.

Col brought an herbal infusion and in moments it settled her stomach, not that she thought she would be able to be sick again; she had already lost her breakfast. Michael refused lunch, not wanting to leave her side, dismissing with a shake of his head her insistence that he eat something.

She recognised the consideration; it belonged to the old Michael. That was how he had been, kind and considerate. When she had had a cold, he had taken charge of everything. He had looked after her wonderfully well. She had felt treasured and adored. Obviously those traits were still there inside him; he had not managed to choke them out of himself. There was a little comfort in realising that.

She thought she felt stronger when they reached Miami, yet her legs felt unsteady; however, Michael had his arm firmly around her as they crossed the tarmac and it was not far to walk to a waiting car. The hotel they arrived at she recognised as being in the Hernandez group.

She anticipated, with a certain amount of dread, there would be a fuss when they realised the big boss had arrived, but surprisingly it was no more than was offered to any other guest. She guessed this was Michael's dictate and not the staff's. There was no need to register at the desk and very soon the elevator whisked them up to the penthouse suite. The suite was practically as large as the apartment in New York. It was furnished in a similar style and when she asked if Michael let it to guests, she was not surprised when he said he did not. It was very much a home.

There was a wide terrace and on Michael's advice she went and sat out there beneath a shady umbrella. She had not been there for longer than ten minutes when someone arrived with a pot of tea and some thin slices of toast. Her stomach had settled and seemed prepared to accept both.

When she went inside, Michael was on the telephone. He turned and when he saw she had come in abruptly ended the conversation. Insecurity made her wonder if he had been speaking to a woman but she forced the suspicion to one side. Besides, she was his wife but she was not his keeper. Their vows were vows of convenience; he owed her no fidelity.

"You look terrible!" He said, with such vehemence she stepped back. "Hey hold on, honey," he was at her side, catching her arm as if he thought she would fall. "I didn't mean it as a criticism," he said. "But as a fact and I don't like it. I'm going to call the doctor."

"Oh, there's no need, really I'm fine."

"You might think you're fine but you don't look fine. "

"I don't want to bother anyone."

"Honey, the money I pay the doctor to look after my hotel, she can afford to be inconvenienced. You go lie down, and I'll call her."

She thought it a fuss over nothing more than air sickness, but she knew Michael when he got something into his head. There was no making him change his mind. Besides, she had not the energy to protest too much.

Once in the bedroom, she slipped out of her dress and into a dressing gown, then she went and lay on top of the bed. The toast, tea and Col's herbal infusion had really settled her stomach and apart from feeling exhausted she did not really feel ill. But she had to admit, she had never had this feeling before and it was not like her. It could be the change of climate, she reasoned, or some toxic bug that had given her a nip when she was not aware.

She had had a run-in with a gang of marauding mosquitoes when she had gone out into the garden at the Florida house. Believing she could stroll with impunity amongst the flowers and by the side of the lake, one evening, she took her time. It was only when Michael had come out to rescue her and then doused her in some foul smelling concoction, she realised the air was filled with the pesky insects. It could be those, she supposed.

The doctor arrived, a no-nonsense type of woman of about fifty. Charley was glad it was a woman because she was given a thorough examination, even down to blood being taken.

The woman studied Charley a long time, arms folded across her chest, taking in her pale complexion. She had looked in her eyes with a little light and had her say aah, sounded her chest and felt around her stomach area for, Charley assumed, any lumps.

"Mrs Hernandez, could you be pregnant?"

"Pregnant? Oh no, not pregnant."

"You're sure."

"Absolutely, I had a period."

"When was that?"

"Last time... err," she remembered, it was just before they left for Florida... a couple of weeks ago, just about. When Michael had been staying away from her and she had those long days and evenings to herself.

"Was it a usual period, anything different about it?"

"Not really, just a little shorter than the usual one, not quite three days when usually it's four, give or take." Charley shrugged, knowing these questions were such a waste of time; Michael was no fool when it came to protection anyway.

"I can take a sample of your water but why don't we do a pregnancy test just in case?"

Charley sighed and gave her grudging consent. The doctor had a kit with her. Charley thought it odd that a doctor would carry such equipment when you could buy it over the counter at any chemist and drug store, or had Michael relayed her symptoms to the doctor and she had thought to be on the safe side? Forward planning, the mark of a good doctor, Charley supposed, covering all the bases.

"You know," Charley murmured with uncharacteristic rudeness, "this is such a waste of time."

~ * ~

Charley left the bed and went into the bathroom. Stripping off the dressing gown, she stepped into the shower cabin and turned on the mixer taps. The water came out just right, warm and comforting. She just stood under the power spray, letting it soak into her hair and run down her body.

Michael called her name; she heard him above the noise of the shower, the glass patterned so he would see her outline.

"I won't be long," she called. She prayed please don't come in, don't open the door, don't do it, Michael, please. He called something which must have meant that he was leaving her on her own, for she heard the door close.

She unscrewed the cap from the shampoo and poured some into her palm, washed her hair and then took up the shower gel, well aware of what she was doing. Playing for time, she called it in her mind, not wanting to face Michael.

Mad ideas swept in and out of her mind, schemes and plots and lies and mainly, how she could escape. Just leave the hotel, take a cab and have it take her to the airport; once there she could catch the first available plane to... anywhere.

This was the worst possible thing that could have happened, and she did not even know how it had happened. Furthermore, why had there been no warning, when escape would have been possible? Now it was going to be difficult. Michael. Michael was trapped and he did not wish to be trapped or tied to her permanently. Would he think she had planned it? Yet how could he think that when he had taken responsibility for it not happening.

She did not know how she felt about it either. Turning off the jets, she slid onto the little seat in the corner of the shower; postponing the inevitable, leaving her hair dripping down onto her wet shoulders, the trickle of water irritating. She put up her hand and squeezed her hair free of some of the wetness. Prevarication was not an answer. She left the stool and, opening the door, stepped into the bathroom. Taking up a towel, Charley patted her body dry, wrapping a towel around her head before slipping into the robe she had hung behind the bathroom door.

The bed had been straightened. A night dress lay across her pillow, dark cream satin. She went and lifted it, holding it against her, the satin folds sliding against her hands. It had tiny silk shoe string straps and lighter cream lace cups at the chest; it had that brand new smell so she knew Michael had bought it for her. Oh hell, she thought, sinking onto the bed and pushing the night gown to one side.

She had not unpacked and her case was on a stand. She opened it and pulled out a dress that was on top, merely a silk shift cool and comfortable. She found a pair of white silk panties and matching bra and pulled these on, tugging the dress over her head. She had forgotten the towel was wrapped around her hair, and had to struggle to remove it before carrying on. Without putting anything on her feet, she slid miserably across the carpet, briefly combed her hair and then slumped out into the lounge area.

Michael was sitting on the terrace; he had not changed or shaved or showered, but had just cast aside his jacket and tie and rolled up his sleeves. The moment he heard her, he jumped up from the chair and came to her side, taking up her hand and very gently kissing the palm.

"How are you?" His eyes searched her face, the look so deep she felt herself colour up, unable to meet his gaze. She folded her hand into his, just for a moment and then released her hold and stepped back.

"Michael," she said, feeling shamefaced and just then, in spite of his worried look, so terribly alone. This being that had invaded her body, and that was how she thought of it just then, was about to drive a wedge between them. It would bring down their tenuous relationship. Such a relationship could not sustain a blow like this. It was not even a relationship they shared. It was all to do with the sexual attraction neither of them had been able to push to one side, but this would finally do that. No man wanted to be trapped with a woman he neither respected nor loved, that much she knew.

"So?" he asked, he looked like he wanted to smile but something about her seemed to be preventing him. "Don't keep me in suspense, babe, what did the doctor say? Are you okay? Nothing too serious, is it? She said that. I pay the woman but she would tell me nothing apart from that. Patient confidentiality... 'Hey, I'm her husband, I said.' Come on, Charley, this is killing me." But he spoke kindly and if he was irritated with the doctor's ethical stance, he certainly was not irritated with her, at least not yet.

"Michael..." she hesitated.

He went towards her but saw that she backed away and so stayed where he was. "Charley, you're making me really scared now," he admitted.

"Don't be, Michael. I'm not suffering from a terminal disease or anything like that. It's difficult, so please bear with me."

"Sure," he said, looking now very serious, a frown scarring his perfect brow.

She moistened her lips. "I'm pregnant." The words came out very loud to her ears. Watching him she saw the colour going from his skin; the soft brown became a rather sickly colour, and his face took on a rather haggard look. It was as if she had hit him in the stomach; he looked as if he was reeling from the intensity of it.

"You should have told me," he said at last, very cold and distant.

"I have... I mean I only just found out."

"Oh, really," he said and the way he said it... as if he was calling her a liar. "What I mean exactly, is that you should have told me you were in a relationship, with someone else."

Waves of dizziness threatened to engulf her. There was a chair... stretching out a hand, she clasped it, moving closer to it, so the arm dug into her thigh. It was her support, her crutch.

"Are you okay?" he asked, cool but not without some concern.

"What are you saying, Michael?" she managed. She actually felt the blood draining out of her face, knew she had to look pale. He had hit her back, as she had struck him a blow so, metaphorically speaking, he had retaliated.

"Come on, Charlotte." A bad sign, she thought, his using her full name. There was no bonhomie about him when he used her name in that tone of voice... yet he called her Charlotte when they made love; then she was ever Charlotte to him. She recalled the last time, it was an idiotic memory that had no right to invade her mind at this time, yet it was there. It was vivid and real and wonderful, yet it had nothing to do with this man who now looked at her coldly. There was no warmth in the way he said her name, no sigh of pleasure in the very utterance of it as there had been in the first light of dawn.

"Don't treat me like a naive fool. I'm not that young guy anymore, and I sure as hell did not make you pregnant!"

Another blow, it knocked the very breath from her body. Moving around the chair, she sank onto it. There was a sinking feeling in every part of her and coming up fast, there was the dull ache of pain at her throat and chest. She swallowed the urge to sob. Her sane mind was daring her to stand up, walk away, pack her bag and then leave.

He wanted nothing to do with it; okay then, he would have nothing to do with it. Once she got away she would decide what she would do. She would face this catastrophe on her own, in her own time.

But she could not move, could not speak. She was looking down at her feet; they seemed small, the toes curled defensively, the pretty pastel pink colour of the nails hidden from view. The carpet felt smooth against her bent toes. It was a thick white pile carpet, totally impractical. She would never have such a carpet in a hotel she owned; she would have a patterned carpet. But this was not a hotel room; it was the owner's suite. These silly thoughts danced in and out of her mind in the silence that lay before them. It was Michael who broke into the silence and who sent these inconsequential thoughts winging out of her mind.

"So hadn't you better call him?"

She shot him a glance, her eyes hot now as rage came to her rescue.

"Don't worry, I'll leave the room," he said checking his watch. "It'll be about ten p.m. in England."

"You know, Michael, you must think me a real slut," she said and her voice was cold with rage now. "I just wish I had realised that."

She pulled herself from the chair; rage was a motivational force, it was easy to treat with him while that was burning away inside her.

"Can you blame me, with your pedigree?" he said and he was cold, too. She wondered for a moment if he was in a rage, too but no... he did not care that much about her to get into a rage.

"Michael, one day you're going to regret this. If you'll excuse me, I have to pack."

"At least wait till I get you a flight," he said.

"Michael, it might surprise you to know I don't want you to do anything for me, ever again."

He said nothing. She took a swift look at him and saw he was staring not only at her, but through her. The look of hate seemed to her to be there in his eyes. He really believed it. It was so tragic as to be almost laughable. He believed she had been with other men, that she was having a relationship with Michael while still involved with someone else. Just where did he get such ridiculous ideas?

Then she knew. She saw it all clearly for the very first time. Someone had planted those seeds in his head. As she had been deceived about him so he had been deceived about her. How stupid she was not to have realised that! And she had let him think these things; she had never tried to defend herself. If they had ever talked about the past properly, then it would have all come out, but she was bound by some ridiculous promise to keep his sister's part in their breakup her secret.

She made her way across the carpet. He was on her before she realised it, before she had a chance to slip through the bedroom door and slide the bolt. His hand mangled her arm, not really hurting her, but she still whimpered in protest and he released the firm grip, merely cupping her arm. She had no strength to physically break free of him.

His eyes raked her face; there was something so physical about it. She held her head back from him. Those eyes seemed to tear into her skin; she could feel pain, as if he had slapped her.

"How could you do this... again?" he demanded. "To some other guy as well? God, Charlotte, what kind of woman are you?"

She groaned softly. "If you removed the blinkers and stopped being so prejudiced, you'd know."

"Prejudiced? Is that what this is, this burning inside me, this fury that makes me hot and cold... prejudice? Prejudice I can deal with, your double dealing I can't. I should have known you could never be satisfied with one man, and you know what... I even feel sorry for the other guy."

"Michael," she tilted her chin and even though his eyes boring into her were causing her real agony, she met his gaze. She did not shrink from his damning look. "There is no other man. Now I know you are not going to believe me, so why don't you just let go of my arm and let me leave. That way no one gets hurt any more than they need to."

"And as difficult as it is for you to believe, I took good care of things so you would not get pregnant!" he said, the words spitting from him but they were like icicles, piercing her flesh.

"Then go to the drugstore and ask for your money back."

Her simple statement seemed to take the power from him. He released her arm and stepped back. Her upper arm felt cold now. Unselfconsciously she cupped her hand around it.

"Okay, we'll take a paternity test."

"Michael, you can do what you like but I don't want to be involved in it. I want nothing from you, nothing at all. I have no intention of proving medically what I've said. You can accept my word or you can't. I just don't care anymore. You have your mind made up about me, and nothing I say will ever change your perceptions."

"Perceptions? Oh yeah, perceptions… that's what you call me arriving home and finding you gone and your lover in the apartment we shared."

"I don't know what you are talking about."

"Sure you do. Luke… Luke…" he frowned as if trying to bring a name to mind.

"Luke Carlson?"

"There, the name just trips off your tongue."

~ * ~

Luke Carlson. The name came swimming to the surface of her mind. Funny how the name did just trip off her tongue like that, but then again she had never known any other Luke. Yet what had Luke Carlson to do with them? And why was he at the apartment she had shared with Michael? It did not make sense.

Some of the bafflement must have shown on her face, for Michael stepped back, putting his hand up against the architrave as if he did not trust himself not to manhandle her.

"I don't understand," she said.

"Sure you do," Michael's answer was full of accusation. "You were seeing him all the time we were together. He told me before I lifted him off his feet and shook him, not after!"

That would not be difficult for Michael to do, she thought irrationally. Luke Carlson was as tall as she and just as slender. Michael towered over them both. But she still did not understand why Luke Carlson would be at their apartment after she had left. He was not even a friend of hers; in fact, she really disliked him.

He worked at the diner with her while he paid his way through college and was always asking her out, even when she was going out with Michael. She really thought him rather creepy... there was something sly and mean about him. She had once caught him taking another waitress' tips while he cleaned the table, leaving the girl to think that the customer had stiffed her. Charley had not ratted on him; but she had told him what she knew. She warned him that if she ever saw him do it again, she would go to management. After that his attitude to her changed, he always ignored her, never even spoke, which was in some ways fine by her. But now, Michael was saying he was at their apartment and after she had gone.

"And he said what exactly?"

"I told you what," Michael said.

She smiled a humourless smile. "And you believed him? You have so little worth you think I would go out with someone like him when I had you."

"You'd left. You didn't leave a note but you left him to clear up your mess. He was even packing up the stuff you left behind. He was going to take it to England when he joined you there."

Charley looked at him helplessly, arms at her side. There was an urge now, which she almost gave into, to burst into tears. Not to melt his coldness but to somehow release all the charged up emotion churning away inside of her.

"Oh, Michael," she moaned. "I left the stuff because it was what you bought me. I left it because I didn't want to ever be reminded of you. And as for his being there, I don't know why, or how. I loathed the guy, I thought you knew."

"So you said. But dislike is a pretty good cover, don't you think?"

"I wouldn't know. Excuse me," she pushed past him, going into the bedroom but not closing the door because he was still there in the architrave, though he had brought his arm to his side and when she glanced him, saw he had thrust both hands into his pants pockets.

"You tell me how he got the key then? How he knew you were going to England? That you were leaving?"

She sighed wearily. "I don't know. I went to pick up my pay cheque and to tell them at the diner I was leaving. Maybe someone mentioned it to him. Maybe he wanted to get revenge on me because of that time I caught him taking Sadie's tips, I don't know. Or maybe someone..." she stopped, biting on the words. Her back was towards Michael, she could not bear to look at him anymore, not and see that coldness in his eyes. She knew he was neither lying nor exaggerating. He had to have been devastated to come back to their cosy apartment to discover another man there, and a man that said he was her lover. It was all too easy for him to believe it, if the shoe was on the other foot she would have believed it, too.

"Someone?" The question drifted across to her. He had heard that 'someone' and now wanted her to finish the sentence, yet how could she?

"I don't want to talk about it anymore, Michael. All I'm going to say is Carlson was never my lover. I mean, what would I want with another lover when I had all I could handle at home?"

"I can't see why anyone would do that," he insisted.

"Because it wouldn't enter your head to do anything like that. Who knows why people want to make trouble for others? Jealousy, spitefulness, a lack of something in their lives. Anyway, it's all in the past."

"If you had just gone and I hadn't found him there, I would have come looking for you," he said.

The words hit her where it hurt the most, her heart. All those wasted years and it need not have been. It could have all been sorted out then. He would have found her and she would have been able to tell him what had happened. They would have got through it all and who knew what their future would have been like. There would have been kids and the family would have reunited after a period of animosity. She closed her eyes against the very thought of it.

She heard the door close. Turning she saw Michael had pulled the door closed and he was on the other side of it. Weakly she sank onto the bed; her head started to spin, her heart to accelerate at a frightening pace. Taking deep breaths she waited for it all to pass and it did, after about ten minutes.

There was a knock at the door. Knowing it would not be Michael because he would not have knocked, she called 'come in.' A waiter came in and asked if she would like some tea and something light to eat. Realising the waves of dizziness could be down to an empty stomach and even while not feeling like eating, she ordered toast and a pot of tea.

Realising the sheer futility of packing her bag and going to the airport without a booked flight in her emotional and physical state, she decided to wait until the next day. Michael would organise her flight anyway. He would have more influence in that department and he would be anxious for her departure.

After what seemed like only minutes, the waiter was back wheeling a tray to her side. There was warm buttered toast beneath a napkin; her stomach gave a lurch of appreciation. Slowly she nibbled on a piece of toast. It really was difficult to do for all she really wanted was to curl into a ball and fall into a deep sleep. She needed to shut off her mind but the process would not be helped if she had a yawning emptiness inside her.

In the end, she ate half the toast, pouring herself tea and taking it black. The tea tasted really good; she was parched and had not even been aware of it. Nervously she ran a hand over her stomach. Did all this emotional seesaw she was on hurt the tiny being inside her? Was it curled and frightened, feeling the highs and lows and drowning in the undertow?

After moving the food trolley out of the way, she went and lay on the bed, on her back, taking long breaths, holding the breath and counting in her head, slowly releasing it. The exercise was calming. Then the door opened and Michael stepped into the room. He looked terribly pale and there were lines etched around his mouth. Her heart sank. If he started again to argue with her, she knew she would have to leave, she had no strength. However, he must have assumed that she was sleeping, for he turned around to leave, quietly pushing the trolley out of the room. He managed to whisper the door to a close. There must have been a switch near the door that worked the curtain, for the white chiffon also swished to a close, dimming the room.

She knew she would not sleep; her mind was on fire, thoughts teaming in and out of her consciousness, yet she could, with effort, and by controlling her breathing, relax a little.

For all the years that had gone by, she could have sobbed, for the wasted moments and all the time she had been unhappy and miserable. Now realising Michael had been the same was no consolation. It would be so good, she thought, to just go into the lounge area and confront him. Explain what had happened with regard to his sister and the woman who had pursued him for so many years.

Why should she care what it did to his family? She had her own little life growing inside her to think about. Yet what would be the use? It was too late to go back. They would never recapture what had been stolen from them. It was gone forever and revealing everything would do her, and more importantly, their relationship no good at all.

Eventually leaving the bed and rinsing her face and neck in cool water, she went into the lounge. No one was there; she travelled the suite of rooms but Michael was not there. Only as she tramped across the lounge did she see a note propped up on the writing desk.

Michael's handwriting swam before her eyes, causing her heart to plummet even before she read what was written. Imagining it would be some kind of ultimatum, she fully expected there to be airline tickets on the desk. She looked for these before she even read the note. There was nothing on the desk but the letter.

Charley, it began, not even dear Charley she noted —

I have to go to the Bahamas today. There is no way I can get out of it. I intend to sort out my business there very quickly and should be back tomorrow, or the day after. I would like you to wait until I get back. Believe me, if this business was not really urgent I would not go. There is no way I can sort it out other than by going.

I've instructed the staff to look after you. If you want anything just ring the desk—I've also left car keys if you want to drive anywhere, alternatively the desk clerk will arrange for a car with driver. Try to enjoy Miami. I am sorry, I just have to go, and it isn't an option. Michael

She read the note three times, feeling she had missed something. It was very matter of fact, no mention of her pregnancy, or their argument. It was the kind of letter he probably left for any girlfriend he had, or the sort of thing he would do for any guest of his.

The idea she could go wandering around Miami like a tourist was ridiculous. Did he imagine she was a person without any feeling? He had verbally abused her, telling her he did not believe the child she had conceived was his! He implied she was some kind of slut who went from man to man without a care for the consequences. After doing his worst, he expected her to just... enjoy herself.

The truth was... the thing that really hurt was there was no apology for that in the letter. The apology was just because he had to leave! If there had been a hint there that he had been wrong she would have seen sense in his telling her to try and have a pleasant time. Casting the letter to one side, she went out onto the balcony and sat in one of the comfy chairs.

Far away she could hear the sound of people at a swimming pool; the wall around the balcony was pretty high but she could just about see over, and sure enough, way below was a huge turquoise pool. Guests were in the water or lazing by the side. However it had no appeal for her.

She had to have dozed lightly, for she awoke to hear a telephone ringing. She got up from the chair hurriedly and staggered a little on her way to the lounge.

"Hello?"

"Mrs Hernandez?" a voice asked. She thought to say no but then realised how stupid that was, for better or worse, at the moment, that was who she was.

"Yes?"

"I have a call for you, one moment please..."

"Who...?" she began, but the operator had gone and before she could wonder about whom the caller was, a voice rang out in the void. It was Dolores.

"Michael's gone to the Bahamas," Charley informed his sister. "You only missed him by..." she checked her watch; she was surprised to see she had to be dozing for about an hour. "Three hours, I guess."

"That's not a problem. I want to come over for the weekend. Charley, is that okay? I'd like to stay till Tuesday."

"If it's all right with your mother I don't see why you shouldn't come. There's loads of room."

"I know that, Charley, I've been before," but the words were spoken humorously rather than snappily.

"Oh, sure you have, sorry, wasn't thinking straight."

It was only as she replaced the receiver Charley wondered what on earth she was doing allowing Dolores to come. It was hardly the right atmosphere in which to bring a young impressionable girl. Yet she admitted to herself she needed the company; having toyed with the idea of just leaving and then realising that would be foolish, it would be good to have company. At least that way she would not be brooding on matters she could do nothing about.

Dolores arrived just before nine that evening. Charley had expected her the next day but she did not say anything about it. The girl looked cool and comfortable in a white linen suit, worn over a black tee shirt. There was no pulling of the neckline or fiddling with the jacket. Dolores was obviously happy with what she was wearing. She also appeared more confident, or perhaps it was that she had got over her initial animosity towards Charley.

"You look terrible, Charley," Dolores announced by way of greeting.

"Thanks, just what I need to boost my ego."

"No seriously, Charley, are you okay?"

"I'll be fine. I just had a little tummy trouble." And you can say that again!

"Are you sure that's all?"

"Of course, now can I get you something to eat or drink?"

"A coke would be fine. I ate on the plane. Say, that jet of Michael's is so cool."

"You used the jet?" Charley was confused. She had assumed Michael had flown to the Bahamas in his own plane and anyway, had not known the private plane had gone back to Tampa.

Dolores blushed. "Oh, oh..." she said, chewing her lower lip. "Don't tell Michael, he will kill me."

"But surely he'll find out. I mean if he sees flight plans and the gas for the plane he'll know, but I won't..."

"No," Dolores waved her hands, "do you imagine I would dare to take his jet without asking? Charley don't you know my brother? I mean this is Michael we're talking about. You don't do things like that to Michael, not if you want to live."

"I'm confused," Charley said.

"I wasn't to tell you... Michael asked me to come."

"He did?"

"Sure, but I wasn't to tell you. He was worried about you. He tried to get out of his trip but he couldn't, so he asked me to come and look after you. Sorry! You won't tell him, will you?"

"Of course I won't."

He was worried about her? Michael was so concerned he had sent the jet for his sister to come and stay with her? She felt sudden warmth flowing through her, and then shook it out of herself. Was she melting just because he had done her a kindness? The way he had treated her he deserved to be worried! Yet there was suddenly a lightness about her and she was not about to chase that away.

"Tomorrow I'll show you the sights," Dolores announced, "Michael said you haven't been to Miami before. Is there anything you would really like to see?"

Charley shrugged. "You know, Dolores, there is, would it be possible to go Key West?"

"Sure, not a problem."

The rather surly hostile girl that Charley had met at Thanksgiving had gone. Instead, this Dolores was as charming as her brother; she was bubbly and kind and informative. There was breeziness about her that Charley could not equate with the girl she had been. The answer to the change was two fold. In the first place, her essential personality was charming. She had been hostile to Charley because she blamed Charley for making her brother so unhappy. The other change came from Michael having a long talk with her mother. Dolores was to be allowed to live near to campus. Michael would buy her a small apartment. That way she would feel more in the swing of things. He would expect good reports, though and promised if her work suffered, then the apartment deal was off.

"I won't let him down," Dolores said. "I want to do well... I mean in the summer break I'll work at one of his hotels out of state. That way I can start learning the business while still at college, then when I graduate I won't have to start right from scratch. I'll have some experience. I mean, I don't mind being a desk clerk at first, but I don't want to be a kitchen porter, you know what I mean?"

"Having been a kitchen porter, Dolores, I know exactly what you mean," Charley said with feeling.

"And you spoke to Michael, so that was kind of you. I really didn't want to like you, Charley, but I think I do like you. Is that okay?"

"That's cool," Charley said.

"Great." Dolores slipped her arm into Charley's. "So let's go see Ernest Hemingway's house."

The day was so busy when they arrived back, neither felt like going out on the town. They ordered dinner in the room and asked for it to be set out on the balcony. It was a beautiful balmy evening. They enjoyed a delicious fresh fruit salad for dessert. It had grown dark and the sky was littered with stars. There was a huge pale gold moon.

Charley declared she had never seen a moon so round and large. It had to be a lucky omen.

That night Charley slept, long and deep. She did not wake, nor lie in abject misery. The day had been exhausting but fun, too, and had temporarily chased away the dull pain that always seemed to sit deep inside her.

When she did waken, it was to hear the sound of soft voices drifting through the slats of the louvered windows.

. She had left the window to the balcony open, only closing the fly screen and the louvers. She left the bed and opened the wooden shutters. She could hear the rumble of voices but unless she stepped out onto her balcony, she could not see who was out there.

Slipping into a silk robe and fastening the ties tightly, she went out into the lounge. Sunlight spilled in from the open doors of the balcony; the clock on the wall above the antique occasional table told her it was turned eleven. Turning to the sound of voices, she saw Dolores. The girl was sitting at the table on the balcony, her back to the room. To her side was Michael. Nervously, Charley put a hand up to her throat hesitating between going back to her room, or going to join them, as she would do in any normal circumstance. The delicious aroma of freshly percolated coffee propelled her legs in the direction of the balcony.

"Good morning," she said hesitantly; Dolores turned her smile warm.

"Hey sleepy, glad you could make the day."

"I'm sorry," Charley murmured, "I had no idea I had slept so long."

"Not a problem, you must have needed it. What do you say, Michael?"

Michael stood, and then pulled out a chair indicating she should join them. The look of him devastated her, so much so she felt she could not even move. In a dark cream suit and an open neck fawn coloured silk shirt, he was as attractive as ever. No man, and knowing the thought was irrational Charley could not help it, should be allowed to look that good.

"Come and sit," he urged warmly. "There's hot rolls, orange juice, coffee."

He studied her carefully; her face had a warm glow... her day with Dolores had done her good, he realised. It had been heart wrenching to have to leave, if there had not been a serious problem at his Bahamian hotel, he would never have left.

Guilt started to rise up in him. It would never leave him and he would never be able to make it up to her. He could not understand why he had to be that way with her. Was it because she had broken his heart? More than that, his rational side counselled and consoled him. She had all but ruined his life. He had lost himself in drink and certainly he was headed for a nervous breakdown. His family had looked on in horror as he had spiralled into a nightmare world.

~ * ~

Charley made it to the table, sliding herself into the chair. Warm rolls, the coffee, each teased her taste buds. Taking up a hot roll, she spread a little honey on it, aware that Michael's arm brushed her own as he poured coffee into her cup.

Michael, she knew, needed to behave normally so his sister did not feel uncomfortable. He smiled at Charley and started talking.

"So you girls had a great day yesterday," he said, as if nothing had happened between them. How cool was that, Charley thought; he was able to behave as if he hadn't shown me how much he really hated me only a day and a half ago. Yet with his sister there, what else could he do? He was not a man who would verbally crucify her in front of anyone, let alone his youngest sister.

"It was fun," Charley admitted, taking a little bite out of the roll, chewing it and then swallowing it before sitting back in relaxed relief when her stomach did not reject it. The coffee, too, went down unhindered. "I loved Key West."

"I'll bet you went to Hemingway's house," he teased, smiling up at her. If he was faking the warmth, then he was being very good at it since he seemed so genuine.

"How did you guess that, Michael?" Dolores asked.

"Charley and American Literature... I know she loves it. Hemingway, Fitzgerald, the poetry of Dickinson."

"Do you really? I guess you never had to read that stuff in high school," Dolores shuddered.

"No, I didn't, I just did it for good old pleasure. Did you have a good trip, Michael?"

"Yes," he poured some more coffee into his cup. "But today I think you should really relax, Charley. You look better but you should take care."

Well obviously! But she did not say anything, merely shrugged her shoulders.

"Hey, Michael, a hint is good enough to me. Now you're back I intend to go and see some friends. In fact I'm going to call them now. See you two love birds later."

In the wake of Dolores' departure they sat in silence. There was a slight rustle but it was Michael shrugging out of his jacket and casually draping it over the back of his chair. He sprang open the three buttons on his shirt, revealing the strong, firm lines of his neck, and the top of his chest, just above where curls of hair began.

"Why did you leave me?" The words were warm and honeyed, not in the least accusatory. There was the faintest hint of pain there, somewhere just below the surface. She turned to face him; his dark eyes seemed to burn right through her. Her fingers curled around her throat; she swallowed, felt the colour flooding her cheeks as she realised she could give him no answer.

"I don't know," she whispered.

"Sure you do," he said, less honeyed but still without accusation. "I just don't get it, all this time I thought, imagined even, you and that little creep," his bitter laugh was more of a grunt. "You know what? I find I employed the bastard. Now isn't that what you English call irony?"

"Employ Luke Carlson but how... where?"

"At the Hernandez Plaza in New York. He was an assistant manager."

"Was? You mean he left?"

"I wouldn't say he left. I would say that metaphorically I kicked his butt all the way up Broadway."

"You sacked him?"

"Bet your..." he shrugged, swallowing the rude expression. "I did. When I think that little creep has been on my payroll for four years and I didn't even know it? What does that say about me?"

"It says you're good at delegation. You trust your managers. But how did you find out?" Then after realising what it implied, she asked "Were you looking for him?"

He pushed the fingers of one hand inside his opened shirt. As if he were warm, he sprung some more buttons. The day was heating up, and there was a faint swell of humidity coming in. "I guess I made a few checks. You can't blame me for that, or can you?"

She made no answer. Was he trying to find Luke Carlson to confirm her story? If he was, then she did not want to know and preferred it not to be confirmed that he had not entirely believed her. Yet he had sacked him. Maybe he did that having taken her word for it, which was a more comfortable thought.

"So what am I going to do about you?" he asked.

Charley sighed; taking up her cup she took a sip of coffee. Just love me, she wanted to say but never could.

"I'm sorry, Charley," he said.

She put down her cup; her hand had started to tremble.

"I should never have spoken to you like I did. I take full responsibility for what has happened."

"Thank you!" It was not how she wanted to say it; it came out sarcastic and yet why not say it like that? He took responsibility; he was accepting the baby was his when there should have been no doubt. Yet with what he believed about her, how could she really blame him for being suspicious, and it was not as if he had wanted to make her pregnant. He had always gone out of his way to ensure that should not happen.

She could feel the tension building between them, tension and a wall of silence. It was a relief when Dolores breezed out onto the terrace to tell them she was leaving for the day. Charley longed to beg her sister-in-law to stay but already she was leaning over her brother and kissing his cheek. On her way past Charley she ran a hand down her head, as if Charley were the younger of the two. "Have a nice day, both of you." Then she was gone, blissfully unaware of the atmosphere between Charley and Michael.

"This is what I think you should do," Michael said at last.

"No," Charley said.

"No to what?"

"To anything, I just don't want you telling me what I should do anymore."

Michael sighed. "Okay, what do you want to do?"

"Thank you for that courtesy, at least," she looked across at him, and then she could not resist a slight smile, to which he raised an eyebrow. "I haven't a clue," she admitted. "I thought of leaving, going back to England," she shrugged. "I don't know what I want." But of course she did, yet she could never tell him.

"If I might suggest," he said and she nodded. "Flying isn't doing you any good. I think you should go back to Tampa and stay there for the duration."

"Oh, really? And then what?"

"That's up to you," he said ambiguously.

"I don't follow," she said.

"I'd like to be around for my child."

A victim of hormones that were spinning wildly out of control. she could not resist saying. "Always assuming it is your child."

"Don't start, Charley, it isn't even funny. I've said I'm sorry. I can't take back what I said… the only thing I can do is apologise and beg you to forgive me. I don't know why it is you make me like that!"

"Don't blame me for how you act," she murmured but kindly. "I know it wasn't funny, what I said. I don't know why I act like that around you either. I'm sorry but, Michael, we have made such a mess of everything."

"I made the mess," he admitted, "and I'm prepared to face that and help." His words were probably meant kindly yet they pierced her heart. Prepared was not the same as wanting, nor did it come anywhere near the essential element, which was love.

"To coin a phrase, it takes two to tango, Michael."

"I didn't have to make love to you, Charley. I made love to you because I wanted to, so…" he shrugged, "we both take the blame if you like, you for being sexy and gorgeous and me for being unable to contain my lust."

"And was that all it meant, Michael, lust?" she dared and then took a deep breath dreading the answer.

"I can't offer anything else, Charley, not unless you level with me. I'd like to trust you, but I …" he stood and went and looked over the balcony, then turning slowly thrust his hands into his trouser pockets, ballooning the silky material. "Charley, I'm sorry. I can't get a handle on why you left and I don't want it in my gut, but I can't get it out. Okay, I got it wrong with Carlson but damn it, Charley, you have to see it from my point of view. I go away for three days, I come back and you've gone… no note, no word, and no address …just gone like you never existed. I don't want to go into that hell again."

Charley stood now, wracked with guilt, aware of his pain. Knowing she could rid him of that pain was terrible because she was so tempted. Yet she had promised and even if he did know the truth, would it really make any difference to their relationship. He wasn't going to fall in love with her once the truth was revealed. If he did not love her now, he was never going to fall in love with her again over a few words.

"I don't feel one hundred percent," she said, "maybe later I'll get that rush of energy I believe pregnant women get, so I would like to stay. The idea of flying to England…" and dealing with the business end of the hotel, but she did not say that. He would not need her to say that; he was no one's fool.

"I tell you what we could do, only if you like… we'll take a slow drive to Tampa. It'll be a pleasant journey for you. You just relax, don't worry about anything. If anyone needs to worry, then let it be me."

"Thank you," she said and she meant it.

"It's not a problem," he said. "How about we leave Tuesday"

Eight

Local people said it was chilly yet she did not feel particularly cold and the pool was heated so she used it every day. She still wore light pants and tee shirts, although when Dolores visited, her sister-in-law was often wearing a fleecy sweatshirt and jeans.

Dolores came once a week, usually on a Thursday. They ate dinner and chatted and then Dolores drove home. She was thrilled about the baby and already had wheedled them both into promising her a role as godparent.

Mrs Hernandez had come once. Michael was home and there was no opportunity for Charley to talk to her mother-in-law on her own. Her attitude to the child was different from Dolores. Dolores brought baby gifts every time she came: little booties, matinee coats, more than one mobile and so many cuddly toys Charley had to tell her to stop. Mrs Hernandez brought no gifts, which was statement enough that she disapproved Charley thought.

Just before Christmas, Maria gave birth to her baby. It was a little boy. The family went to Mexico to see the new addition to the family and stayed over for the holiday. It left her and Michael alone, but Charley was not in the mood for a grand celebration anyway.

The rush of energy everyone said she could expect had not come. She felt dreadful most of the time. Her hair hung limply and her complexion was sallow. Her body felt all wrong somehow and the raging hormones meant that quite often she would snap at people when there was no reason for it. Immediately she apologised.

"Who is this person?" she asked her reflection, "because I want you to go away. I don't like you at all."

There were other times when she longed for Michael. She suffered long into the night the physical agony of burning desire and knew there was nothing she could do about it. She could not even bring herself to go to him, to tease him into submission. He would never desire the person she had become, this lumping miserable, unattractive blob. He did not ever come to their bedroom anymore but stayed in a room at the end of the corridor when he was home.

Christmas had been less than joyful. She found it odd she could swim and sit out in the sun. She was used to the cold Christmas of England and of the North Eastern states. This was so different and even when a tree was delivered, and there were brightly coloured boxes beneath the branches, it felt rather peculiar.

She stirred herself sufficiently to go Christmas shopping at one of Tampa's malls. She had not known what to buy for Michael and in the end had gone for books she knew he would enjoy. The assistant gift-wrapped them for her and they looked quite beautiful. She thought the gift impersonal enough but when she walked by a men's store, she spied a shirt in a shade of blue she knew would look so good on him, she went in and bought him that as well. The gifts for his family she had no trouble in selecting. Charley had always been a pretty good shopper for people and even buying something for Mrs Hernandez did not faze her.

The gifts the family bought for her were obviously chosen after consultation with him. There were a couple of beautiful cashmere sweaters and her favourite perfume and some books.

She left Michael's gift to the last, a long box beautifully wrapped in gold paper. The card merely said. "Charley, Happy Christmas, Love, Michael." It was written in his own hand, so thankfully he had not had one of his secretaries buy the gift. Gingerly she opened the box, carefully removing the paper. It was a black velvet box. With an anxious glance at him, she opened it, sitting back on her heels.

"Michael, I can't take this." The sparkling necklace of diamonds and sapphires twinkled up at her. It was exquisite, the diamonds small and finely cut. "Sure you can," he said. "Shall I put it on?"

She nodded. "Wearing diamonds for breakfast, why not?" she said lightly. His fingers brushed the skin at her neck, awakening a throbbing desire that made her gasp for breath. When he had done, she went to the mirror to look. Even against the pale green of her blouse, the necklace looked fabulous.

"I never had anything like this," she admitted.

"I know," he said, "so enjoy it… hey, Charlotte!" He had been opening his present. "Thank you. What wonderful books!" Hardly comparable, she thought but then again she was not as wealthy as her husband. He liked the shirt too, unselfconsciously pulling the shirt he had on off, and slipping into the new one. She had been so right; it suited him perfectly. Trouble was it only served to make her heart do somersaults.

Two days into the New Year, Charley went to bed earlier than usual. She had felt weary all day, in spite of having had a good night's sleep. Something made her waken; she pulled herself from the deep sleep and held her breath, as if afraid someone was in her room.

There were no sounds. Suddenly she felt it, the thing that had wakened her. A tight band of pain was tearing across her lower abdomen. In her half sleeping state she thought, my period is starting. She started to slide from the bed but the pain came again and she remembered.

There was a warm wetness between her legs. She quickly reached over and pulled the switch on the lamp. The room had flooded with light before another pain assailed her. It was not a trickle she saw, but a flood of crimson, staining the white silk of her night gown.

"Oh… no… I'm sorry…" she cried, unable to move. What had she done? There was an internal phone. She tried to raise herself but couldn't; she pressed seven and five, the number that she had written as being Michael's room, not even knowing that he was there.

There was no reply, then she realised why. The clock said it was only eleven-thirty. If she could get to the door, she could yell and someone would come but she could not seem to move and anyway was afraid to in case it made things worse. She picked up the phone again and jabbed in numbers haphazardly until at last the phone rang out. It was picked up right away and it was Michael.

"Michael, please come... right now... please."

He did not ask why or indeed say anything, but slammed down the phone and was at her side in what seemed like seconds.

"What is it?" he asked as he burst in. When he saw her, he cried out in agony, then eased her back onto the bed and dialled emergency.

"What have I done?" she asked, "Oh, Michael, what have I done wrong?"

~ * ~

It was raining ferociously when they left the hospital. Appropriate, she thought. Consuela came with an umbrella the moment the car pulled up outside the house. Still feeling weak at her limbs, they walked into the house at a slow pace. Michael followed carrying her overnight case.

"I make you nice cup of tea," Consuela promised, "and Ma'am, I so sorry."

"Thank you, Consuela, on both counts," she managed a smile. "I think I'll go in the sitting room for a while."

If she told the truth, she was reluctant to climb the stairs to her bedroom. On the landing she would have to pass what would have been the baby's room. There would be all the things Dolores had bought. She knew she was not ready to face them yet.

Michael joined her and soon Consuela came with the tea and a pot of coffee for Michael, as well as some of the honey cakes Charley loved.

"How are you?" Michael asked for about the tenth time that day.

"I'm okay, just a little weak. Not from… just the other thing." She bit her lip. "I mean the other procedure," she managed, meaning the D and C.

"They want you to be safe," he said.

Her eyes flew to his face but his expression was, as it had been all through these few days, quite unreadable. If he was honest maybe he would say it was for the best. How could they bring a child into their loveless marriage of lies? But she could not think that way; she was in mourning for the life of her baby. As always the thought of all the blood came to her and she shuddered violently. Seeing it, Michael was at her side, his arm around her. He had been so kind but then that was what he was when he wanted to be, kind and supportive, generous with his time.

"Hey," he murmured, hugging her gently to him. "It's a tough call, but we'll get through."

We'll get through it? There is no we she wanted to say, there is just me and then there is you and we are as separate now as we have ever been. I lost my baby, my body rejected my baby and I am to blame. I am the inadequate one. The thoughts she had had only days ago came back to haunt her. The resentment she had felt against the being inside her… she had been over the toilet bowl yet again, throwing up her lunch. She had not been filled with awe and wonder. No, her only emotion had been resentment, and she was too afraid to admit that to the man who had planted his seed. He would never understand.

However, she lay now with her head against his chest, his arms around her. Somehow she felt safe, unhappy but safe which was a strange combination. She lay there a long time, listening to Michael's heart beat at a steady rhythm. The rain thundered against the patio doors, great swathes of water were gushing out of the gutters. The fields beyond the house would be sodden... these inconsequential thoughts kept her from thinking about the momentous thing that had happened to her.

"Michael," she whispered.

"Mm, what is it, honey?"

His hand stroked through her hair very gently, the movement comforting. "Why did it happen?" she asked, knowing all the while he had no answer any more than she had. She thought of the doctor's words at the hospital.

"It can happen with first time pregnancies."

As if that was supposed to be a comfort to her.

"I wish I knew. I ask myself all the time, was it me? Did I do it? Dragging you around the country, losing my temper at you? God, I wish I knew."

She eased herself up, looking at him, noticing how pale he was, how there were lines of fatigue at his mouth and eyes. "Michael, you mustn't blame yourself, it was my fault and it was my inadequacy."

"Of course it wasn't," he insisted gently.

"I was so resentful," she admitted, without stopping any more to think of the consequences. "I hated feeling ill all the time, hated the way my body was. I was looking for all the wonderful feelings but they wouldn't come. Oh, Michael what have I done?"

"You did nothing," he said with feeling. "You had a bad time; you were ill mostly. You were bound to feel resentful, and that's perfectly natural. What you did not have to expect was me in full fury. Hell, I could kick myself!" As if he needed to do some violence, he slammed his fist into the palm of his other hand quite violently.

"Don't do that, Michael." Charley cupped a hand around his arm. "Please, don't do it; it isn't your fault."

"Of course it's my fault!" His eyes were wild in his face; there was so much torment there for her to plainly see. "I knew the baby had to be mine. I just needed to…" he ran a trembling hand through his hair. "Do what I always do, kick out at you. God knows I didn't want to act that way, but I couldn't stop myself from punishing you."

"Punishing me? Michael, believing I left you for someone else, how can I blame you for being so bitter? If we had only talked about it, been up front at the very beginning then it might have been easier. But none of that is to blame for me losing the baby, Michael."

Comforting Michael and convincing him in a strange way ameliorated her pain. She could not bear for him to be suffering as he was. Her love for him awakened all the compassion inside her and now it was she who wrapped her arms around him, and ran her hand through his hair. "We'll get through it, Michael, it will hurt for a long time, but we can get through it."

His haunted eyes met hers. "Don't leave, Charley, just don't leave just yet."

"I'm going nowhere, Michael," she murmured, holding him close, "because I can't do this on my own, no more than you can. We have to do it together."

He brushed his lips very gently against her neck. As he kissed her cheek, he tasted her tears on his tongue. "You cry, Charlotte, you let it all out..." and she did, sobbing against his chest while he held her to him, only moving his hand once or twice to wipe away his own tears.

Truly the pain was there, just under his ribs. It would not go away, would give him no respite or no sleep. He thought of her in agony, on her knees, the blood... his daughter spilling out of her and all because of him. His stupid accusation and ridiculous pride! His desperate need to hurt her back, as if he were some kid in the playground.

Payback time... how the words haunted him. If she had died... the thought was unbearable. He held her to him, realising how frail she felt. He could feel her bones through the warmth of the sweater. Sadness overwhelmed him. He was sad for her, for the loss of their baby girl... the one person he was not sad about was himself.

~ * ~

As the brief Florida winter gave way once more to warm and balmy weather, Charley felt her strength returning. As Michael came and discussed the Bloom Hotel project with her, she was now able to give it all her attention. He brought her swatches and paint cards and she spent hours deciding on colour schemes and what textiles to use. The hotel would be finished in April, as Michael had promised, and there would be a grand opening in the middle of the month.

Dolores still came each Thursday and the younger girl's company was a boon for Charley. She would never forget how, when she went up the stairs and collected enough courage to go to the nursery, to find Dolores had been and taken everything away. It was a thoughtful thing to do and showed in its kindness that Dolores truly had her brother's nature.

The family had rallied around. Even Michael's mother had been kind and having the odd afternoon out with Anna was good therapy. Then sometimes, when Michael was home, they had dinner with Anna and Joe, which further helped both her and Michael to mend.

However, when they were alone, they shared their feelings of loss together and talked openly about how each felt. This openness also aided the healing process for both of them. In their grief they were united as one. They knew the baby had been a girl and they gave her a name so they would never forget. They named her Johanna and now when they talked of their loss, they were able to name her, rather than just use the words "our baby."

"I thought of what we could do," Michael said, when he agreed with her choice of colour and fabric for Blooms. "We can go to New York sort of mid-March and have a couple of weeks before we go to England. What do you think?"

"I'd love it," she murmured, trying to sound enthusiastic. The thought of her going back to England permanently was obviously on his mind. This sharing of grief could not go on forever. There had to come the dreaded parting, yet why did it fill her with such horror?

She had known there was no real future between them, had not even expected there to be one.

"Charlotte," at the use of her full name she looked up. Her heart turned over but with misery rather than pleasure. It was time to be serious and real.

"Yes?" she tried a smile; it trembled and died on her lips.

Michael shoved his hands into the pockets of his jacket. He looked as always so immaculate in a dark navy suit. He was wearing the blue shirt she had bought him which had pleased her when he had first come in.

"This is difficult for me," he said.

"Michael, let me make it easier for you. You want me to go back to England?"

"Sure, I want you to go back to England; I want you to be at the opening."

"No, I mean to take up where I left off, running Blooms, like we agreed."

He frowned a little. She saw the firmness come back into his expression. "Do you want to do that?" he asked.

"I thought that's what you wanted me to do," she said, confused now.

"Do you want to?" he persisted.

"Michael, I…"

What to say? If she said no, would he take it she did not want to run the hotel now and she would sell out? Granted it would be a little awkward at first, with her running the hotel, but then he would not be around that much, not if she was running the hotel well and paying back his investment successfully. How often would she see him, twice a year at that? Michael was brilliant at delegating. He knew when to let management run things. Maybe she could make it that they never met, for meeting him would be an agony and a reminder of all the things she hoped for. It would as well remind him of their shared past that one day he would surely wish to forget.

"Look, I'm going to be straight with you," he said so sternly she felt a frisson of fear.

Was he going to tell her he did not think she was up to the job? Would it be a double rejection? Yet, how could he do that? He had only twenty-five percent interest in the hotel, he could not do it. However, if he said he did not think she would succeed, Charley knew she would accept it. She had no strength to do battle with him anymore. Besides if Michael made that decision, it would be because he really believed it and not out of any sense of revenge.

"Please be totally honest," she said. Her hair had grown longer again, and she wore it in a pony tail. Out of nervousness, she pulled the band from her hair and let it fall about her, brushing a trembling hand through the undulating waves.

"I don't want you to run Blooms." Her heart sank. Weakly she left the sofa where she had been sitting, and clasping her hands in front of her she tried to remain calm. She did not want him to see how the blow had devastated her. Pushing her head a little forward Charley made it so her hair would cover her face. She sought around for something to say, and then he spoke again. "I want you to run me!"

"Michael?" she questioned, unsure she had heard right. Surely she was hearing things, he wanted her to run him, and to be with him... was that what he meant?

"I don't want you to leave me. I don't want pretend, I want for real."

"For real? Michael, you mean..." she stepped forward. "The deal is off?"

"That's what I want but if you don't want it, then..."

"Oh, Michael." She went and slid into his arms, pulling him close to her. "I don't ever want to leave you, don't you know that yet?"

He could have said, so easily, but you did leave me, once before, but he didn't. He held her to him in a deep and caring embrace that told her all she needed to know.

"I don't want pretend, honey, I want for real. Do you understand what I'm saying? We're not kids anymore; we can do it this time, can't we?"

"I love you," she murmured against his cheek, standing on tiptoe to press her lips very softly to his.

"I love you too, so very much. I never stopped loving you, which was my problem."

"Kiss me then, kiss me like you really mean it, Michael..."

~ * ~

Later, in the after glow, she held him close to her breast, sighing contentment, relishing the way his mouth cupped the peak of her breast, loving being in his mouth even after the rising passion that had enveloped them.

He was murmuring words to her, talking about her, telling her how he felt about her. She felt warm and full of love. He talked about the first time they had met... he had seen her at the diner... that dark brown hair and the pale green uniform that made the other girls look rather seasick, but made her look like... well, beautiful.

"I know you thought I just wanted to make you, but I knew, right there and then I wanted you and not just for..." he slid his hand against her breast to where his mouth had been, in a slow caressing movement. "But for keeps, you know, no girl made me feel like that, no girl ever has..."

"Oh, Michael, darling. I'm so sorry you were hurt... but... " she knew she had to do it. She had to take away for sure all that pain he had suffered, had to let him know the truth. It was the only way because this time it was going to be for keeps and that meant never having secrets. There would be no more lies and deceit. "Some while ago I made a promise to someone. I want to break that promise but I want something from you in return."

"This sounds vaguely ominous," he murmured, moving from her to lean on his elbow and look down at her. She took hold of the caressing hand, selected a finger and slid it in her mouth, slowly and sensuously. "Are we talking or are we going to..." he asked his voice dark and husky.

She released the finger, snuggled into the crook of his arm and said. "We talk," she said. "Michael, when I tell you something I want you to swear you won't do anything about it and like me, you just let it go. We have to make ourselves do that, Michael, else it won't do either of us any good."

"Angel, I could promise you anything just now, but before I do, you have to give me a hint what it's about."

"It's about why I left you."

He pulled himself up, pumped up a pillow and rested his head against it. "I'm not sure," he said. "I think I'd rather not know."

She knew the only way they could be truly happy together were if he knew the truth. For a while she had had the urge to reveal everything but she had stopped herself. Only now that she knew he really loved her did she realise that it would always be there between them.

Her unjustifiable desertion and how it had broken his heart. She knew that now, he had not told her that exactly but Dolores had. Dolores had told her about the weeks, even months, of depression. Of his inability to do anything, how they feared he would never be the Michael they knew and loved but be a shell of himself. Now she wanted him to deal with her this time on her terms. The one thing she knew for certain was she wanted to go on with their lives but with a slate wiped clean. No lies, no deceit, no avoidance of the truth. There would, she knew, always be that worry in Michael's mind that she had left him once and could do so again. She did not want him to be experiencing any uncertainty.

"I never wanted to leave you, Michael. I loved you then as I love you now. I've never loved anyone else since then."

"Come here," he pulled her up from where she lay, comfortably across his stomach. He plumped a pillow for her and made her sit up. "This is serious business and while you are down there I can't concentrate. I have to promise not to do anything or say anything, is that right? I might want to punch someone's lights out but I haven't to do it, right?"

"Right."

"Tough call, honey."

"We have everything going for us, Michael. We've been through really bad times; nothing can ever be as bad as losing Johanna."

"I guess not, but losing eight years with you comes pretty close."

"Please," she implored, taking up his hand.

He sighed, rubbed a hand across his chest, disturbing the curling dark hair. "Okay, but when you've told me, I have a feeling I am going to need to do something... like go for a run."

"Whatever you want, Michael, the reason I left you was..."

~ * ~

Michael ran. He had pulled on sweatpants and he ran, down the stairs, out of the house... he ran down the drive, out of the gate and along the lane. He ran through muddy puddles but he did not stop or avoid them, he did not even see them. Her words had opened it all up again, just when he thought it was gone. His mother, his sister, Mercedes Mendoza. They knew what they had done. They had watched him nearly lose his mind, saw him on the path to hell and did nothing. How could he do as Charley asked? How could he not say anything?

He ran on, cut off through the woods, jumping fallen logs, dodging bushes, trying to pound the pain out of him. He came to the back of the house, leaned against the wall, bent his knees and bowed his head. His heartbeat slowed.

He could remember the joy he had found with Charley; a blissful happiness he had never known.

Charley, who was so very different from his rather cold mother and autocratic father. A girl very different from his sister, Maria, too. Joe was the only one in the family he had really liked at that time. Charley had made him realise just what real love could be like and they had taken it away from him. Never would he forgive them!

Thoughts of Charley flooded through him. There was her pain, too, she told him about that. How she had had to get over it, not having the comfort of money, how she had worked hard to get where she was. All the time she had to carry her own heartbreak. Yet she had not changed. Essentially she was the same Charley, whereas he had let bitterness chew him up, so much so that he had treated her badly. When he thought of his cavalier attitude towards her, he almost gagged.

Yet she asked him to forgive them, not to do or say anything. Could he do that? What had she said?

"We have a glorious future, Michael darling. We lost years but we can start over and it is just like those eight lost years never existed. We won't let them spoil everything by having family feuds. They did it, they got away with it but now it's gone. Whatever we do we can't get back that lost time but we can make up for it. Our love will allow us to be generous."

He straightened up, jogged around the wall till he came to the front gate. He touched the key pad and when the gates opened, he sprinted up the driveway. He needed to be with the woman he loved and nothing else mattered anymore.

~ * ~

Michael arrived back after an hour, drenched in sweat, from his run. Going into the shower and running it cold, he fought the fury inside him.

Charley was sitting on the balcony where he had left her. She had understood his need. He had to get all the anger out of himself, better he do it now than at a later date, because then it could fester and one day explode.

"Charley," he called. She stood and left the balcony coming into the bedroom. He looked good, she thought, even considering everything. The towel about his waist emphasised his attractive maleness.

"I want you to promise me something now," he said sternly.

"Anything," she said.

"That if anyone and I mean anyone, ever says anything about me again, then you come and you ask me. You don't run and you don't believe and you always, always know I love you more than I could ever love anyone. Family or otherwise."

"Michael…" she ran into his arms. "And that goes for me, too."

"We both went through years of hell because we did not know how to talk to one another and that is never going to happen again, is it?"

"Never." She stood on tiptoe and pressed her lips to his. "And I mean never."

He bent slightly, swept her up into his arms. "My angel," he said, "is back where she has always belonged!"

"And that, my darling, is where she has always wanted to be!"

Meet

Margaret Blake

Margaret Blake was born in Manchester, England and has been writing romance and historical romance for thirty years. Margaret is married to John and has one son and three gorgeous grandchildren and a super daughter in law.